Amish Love Triangle

Monica Marks

Published by Trellis Publishing, 2021.

AMISH LOVE TRIANGLE

First edition. July 13, 2021.

Written by Monica Marks.

AN AMISH LOVE TRIANGLE

MONICA MARKS

It was a blustery but warm day when Jacob arrived at the community center. He entered the doorway in a gust of air, blowing leaves into the entranceway along with him.

"Ah, Mr. Morley," Cathy, the receptionist called, batting her eyes in the flirtatious manner which she deemed becoming. "I see you didn't get blown away out there."

"Nee," Jacob replied but he did reach up to steady his hat which had fallen over his dark head of hair. A long, stray wisp tickled under his nose and for an embarrassing second, he thought he might sneeze. Managing to stifle the attack, he moved toward the west hall where the after school class would be filtering in for care.

"Mr. Morley?" Cathy called after him, her nasally voice causing the hairs on his neck to stand up on end.

"Yes?"

"I was wondering if you were going to attend the parent-care worker party on Friday?"

There was no mistaking the undertone of her voice, the desperation to hear him say "yes" almost tangible.

"I had not considered it," Jacob replied truthfully. Yet as the words left his lips, he thought about who would be in attendance.

Jacob had taken the job at the community center as a way to supplement his family's failing carpentry business. Jacob himself had never had a knack for woodworking, not the way his brother and father had. They had a small piece of land on the outskirts of the district, one which his sister Eliza tended to without the need of an extra hand, leaving Jacob feeling somewhat out of sorts.

He had not expected to enjoy working among the Englisch as much as he did nor did he realize just how much he treasured the children in the community but if Jacob had to guess his primary reason for staying on in his role as caregiver for the after-school program, it would be Ivy Bontrager.

She was the mother of David Bontrager, one of the only two Amish children to attend the center. There was no reason for any Amish child to require such a service, not when the district tended to their own but Ivy had worked in town for several years and David had made friends with the local children. He begged his mother to allow to attend the afterschool program and Ivy had permitted it, likely with convenience in mind. It was easy for her to leave her cleaning job nearby and collect her son on her way home for the day.

Or so Jacob assumed. It was difficult to know what Ivy Bontrager thought when she rarely paid him any mind but to offer him a curt "Danke" when picking up her son.

No one would know we lived only a mile from one another, Jacob thought miserably. *We may as well be strangers.*

"Hello?" Cathy called in a singsong voice, her pitch even higher than before. Jacob likened the noise to nails on a blackboard.

"What is it?" he asked, realizing that she must have asked something which he did not acknowledge.

"I said..."Cathy sighed. "It's going to be great! They're springing on a banquet hall, having a dinner and everything! They never do stuff like that."

"I see."

He knew Cathy was hoping he would agree to accompany her but Jacob could not imagine spending an evening pinned to the chubby blonde's side. She was unbearable enough seeing her in passing.

"It sounds wonderful," he finished lamely, unsure of what else to say. Cathy's face fell but before she could force the issue, the entranceway opened again in a blast of wind and a gaggle of children entered. Jacob exhaled in relief. He did not need to make an excuse to walk away. His work was calling him.

"Hi Mr. Morley!" the kids chanted and he nodded stoically, following them toward the auditorium.

"Think about it!" Cathy yelled after him and he cringed at her shamelessness.

In front of the children!

But as he made his way toward the group, he suddenly wondered if he didn't act the same way whenever Ivy Bontrager was nearby. The idea filled him with shock and disgust.

No! he thought, mortified. *I have never acted so brazenly!*

Yet he couldn't shake the feeling that he was wrong.

~ ~ ~

Ivy was exhausted, her eyes bleary and red from the double shift she had worked at the motel. It was not her first choice in jobs but she had little other choice after the death of her husband, two years earlier.

Joseph had moved her from her district in Indiana to their farm in Ohio but it had not dawned on Ivy that she would be in constant competition for rights to their property when she uprooted her life. Joseph's mother and sister who also lived in the house had made it clear to her from the day they were wed that Ivy was an outsider, despite their common heritage.

When Joseph had passed, succumbing to a cancer which he had kept secret from her, Ivy had been faced with two choices—returning home to Indiana with her young son or remaining in Holmes County. It had been a terrible option. Ivy had wanted nothing more than to scoop up David and never look back toward the pinched faces of her embittered in-laws but it would not be fair to her child to make such a move, not when he adored his father's family.

So, Ivy had decided to stay but she promptly removed herself from the house she had shared with Joseph and found a home in the Schmidt's coach house but she had been forced to find work outside the district to pay their rent. It had been a disheartening couple years for Ivy but things had begun to look up for her when Gideon Byler found himself single.

Now it is a matter of getting him to notice me, she thought as she approached the community center to pick up her son.

As always, she among the last of the parents to retrieve her child, her shift ending at six o'clock and the community center's program finishing at six thirty. It was very near that time when she rushed inside the building, the wind pushing her through the front doors with force.

The receptionist had left for the evening and when Ivy entered the auditorium, she saw that David was the only boy remaining. Jacob Morley tossed a basketball to him and Ivy paused to watch them at play for a moment.

She tried to recall a time when Joseph had ever shown so much attention to David. Her late husband's concern had always been with keeping his mother and sister happy, their son's well-being always the least of his concerns.

Or perhaps my well-being was the least of his concerns.

Abruptly, Jacob turned to look at her as if he felt her dark eyes on him. Instantly, his green eyes brightened.

"Ivy!" he exclaimed in a manner which suggested he hadn't just seen her the previous evening.

"Am I late?" she asked, extending a hand toward David who skipped toward her happily.

"Mammi!"

"Nee, of course you aren't late," Jacob replied, hurrying to join her. "I will always wait for you."

There was a plaintive note in his voice but Ivy barely noticed and she ushered David toward his belongings on the side of the gym.

"Ivy, I am happy to bring David home with me if you would prefer to return straight from work. It is on the way."

Ivy flashed him a quick look and shook her blonde braid, the black straps of her prayer bonnet shifting as she moved, creating a dramatic contrast against her fine straw-colored mane.

"Danke Jacob but this is truly the best part of my day."

She gestured for David to follow and they walked toward the doors, Ivy's mind already on the evening ahead. There was worship that weekend and Ivy was looking forward to seeing Gideon. It was one of the only places she managed to see him with her hectic schedule. She had been working on a special dress for the occasion.

This Sunday, I will be bold and approach him, she told herself firmly. She had almost forgotten about Jacob and she had almost reached the front doors when his voice rang out and startled her.

"Will you be attending the parent-caregiver event on Friday?"

She started slightly and turned back to look at him, her brow knit in confusion.

"I had not heard of any such event," she replied.

"Ja, Mammi, I told you," David insisted. "It will be a party for the grown-ups."

Ivy could not recall and such conversation but that did not mean it hadn't happened. She was simply overwhelmed with work and thoughts of Gideon. Ivy smiled thinly.

"I would not be able to attend such an event," she replied. "Who would watch David?"

"Grossmammi," David replied easily. "We have already discussed it. She thinks you should be looking for a husband. She doesn't think it is natural for a good Amish woman to be working among the Englisch when she is young enough to find a husband to care for."

Ivy's face flushed crimson with humiliation and she chomped on the insides of her cheeks to voice her counter to Iris Bontrager's opinion.

"Ah," Jacob said happily. "It is settled. Shall I pick you up? The party begins at eight o'clock."

Ivy shook her head, casting her son a warning look but he was already flittering toward the exit, oblivious to the effect his parroting had had on his mother.

"Nee," Ivy said quickly. "I have to work on Friday and I cannot say for certain if I will attend. Danke for the offer but perhaps I will see you there."

She did not wait for him to respond and turned to leave before Jacob could press her any further.

"Gut'n owed."

Ivy met up with David and the two approached her cart. She was barely aware of the wistful way he stared after her. Her main concern was escaping the air of embarrassment which seemed to enshroud her.

"David, you cannot repeat Grossmammi's or Rachel's words in front of strangers," she chided the boy as they moved the horse out of the parking lot of the community center. "You should know better than that."

David blinked at her with confused brown eyes, not unlike her own.

"Strangers?" he repeated. "Jacob is a *freind*."

Ivy scowled slightly.

"Nee! He is merely a caregiver. He is not someone we know well. You must be more cautious about who you speak so freely around."

Ivy didn't add that she thought her mother-in-law was a busybody and had no business offering her own advice, especially to a boy so young.

"Nee!" David retorted, much to Ivy's surprise. "He is my *freind* and I can talk to him!"

Ivy was stunned by the backtalk. David was never one to speak harshly. Moreover, the blonde had no idea that her son had developed such an affinity toward the man. For her part, Jacob Morley was merely a common face she saw. She had never given him much of a second thought, despite his attractiveness.

As the rode home against the darkening autumn sky, Ivy found herself wondering why it was she had never much paid him any mind.

He was only a few years older than her but he had never been married, at least not to Ivy's knowledge.

I wonder why that is.

He was certainly handsome enough for any woman and pleasant.

Apparently he has a way with children. Perhaps there is something about him beneath the surface which I cannot see.

"I would still prefer you do not discuss our *familye* matters outside the *familye*," Ivy finally said.

"Mammi, will you remarry?"

The question was unexpected and Ivy inhaled sharply.

"Perhaps. Does that trouble you?" She glanced at him through her peripheral vision, trying to gauge his expression.

"Nee," David replied, surprising her once more. "I think you should marry someone who paid more attention to you than Daed did."

Ivy felt a fusion of pride and worry stab her heart.

"You must not speak ill of your *vedder*," she told him softly but she was equally touched that he had noticed her father's indifference, even though he was so young.

"I only wish for you to be happy, Mammi," David sighed. "If you decide to remarry, please make sure that he is kind to you and puts you first."

"I will," Ivy promised and impulsively reached out to stroke his soft cheek with her hand. "You are a good boy, liebling. You must not worry about me."

David's eyes met hers and he smiled.

"I would not have to if your married someone like Jacob Morley," he replied wickedly and Ivy wondered if her heart would be able to sustain many more shocks for one day.

~ ~ ~

On Wednesday evening, Jacob stopped at a donut shop he enjoyed for a cup of kaffi and a snack. He was far too late to join his familye for supper and while his sister inevitably set aside a plate of food for him, Jacob welcomed the time to himself.

It was becoming abundantly clear that Ivy had no interest in him romantically and Jacob knew that he should give up the idea of becoming involved with her but he couldn't just let it go. He had pined for her for such a long while that he wouldn't even know how to walk away from such an infatuation.

"You seem lost in thought, Jacob," Matthew King announced from the end of the table. Jacob looked up at him, slightly taken aback to see him standing there. He had not realized the man had approached.

"I must be tired," Jacob replied and gestured for the deacon to join him. "Please, sit, Matthew."

The older man joined him in the booth and smiled kindly.

"I might be presumptuous but I think you have something else on your mind than sleep."

Heat rose through Jacob's neck and he lowered his green eyes guiltily.

"Do I read like a book?" he muttered and Matthew laughed.

"You forget I have known you a long while," he reminded the caregiver. "Is it a woman?"

Jacob sighed and nodded.

"Ja but it is an issue which has no happy ending, I fear."

"You never know what Gotte has planned for us," Matthew replied. "Who is the lucky woman?"

Jacob paused, uncertain if he should bare his soul to the deacon but he wondered why not. Matthew was a good friend to the familye and an elder in the church. Whatever Jacob said to him would be kept in confidence and it would be good to share his woes with someone.

"Ivy Bontrager," he confessed before he could change his mind. "I care for her son David in the afternoons at the community center but I do not think she sees me as anything but an instructor to her son."

"Have you spoken to her privately?"

Jacob shook his head.

"I only see her when she comes to pick up David and it is not appropriate at that time."

Matthew frowned at the conundrum.

"Surely, there must be a time when you can see her alone?"

"There is a party hosted by the community center this Friday. I asked her if she will be in attendance but I did not receive a confirmation."

Matthew's eyes lit up.

"That is good news!" he replied. "You will go with a date."

Jacob stared at him blankly, wondering if the deacon had misunderstood his problem but before he could reiterate, Matthew continued to speak.

"Sometimes, all women need to see what is before them is healthy competition. It seems to me that Ivy simply needs her eyes opened in this matter."

Jacob was not certain that attempting to inspire jealousy was the soundest way to get the widowed woman's attention and said as much to Matthew.

"What harm can it do?" Matthew insisted. "You said yourself that you are not certain she will even attend. Would you rather go alone and be without companionship all evening if she does not go?"

Reluctantly, Jacob agreed with the idea but that posed another question.

"Who would I bring as my date?"

"I know just the young lady!" Matthew grinned and leaned forward, his hazel eyes sparkling. "She will be pleased to accompany you to the party on Friday night."

~ ~ ~

Ivy shifted uncomfortably from one foot to another. In her hands was a cup of punch which someone had made with much too much sugar for her liking but she did not like to waste and there was nowhere nearby to set it down. She regretted coming but David had been correct when he claimed his grandmother was coming to watch him and when Iris had appeared at the door on Friday evening after they had returned from town, Ivy had little choice but the permit her entry and ready herself for the party.

In the back of her mind, David's words echoed and over the past few days, she wondered if there wasn't some validity to his innocent remarks about Jacob Morley.

Have I been so infatuated with the idea of Gideon that I did not notice a good man right before my eyes?

She began to think back on all the times she had spoken to Jacob over the past two years and suddenly it became clear that he had been trying to capture her attention all along. How many times had he tried to walk her out of the community center or engage her in conversation? How many looks of yearning had he cast her which she simply dismissed without notice?

Have I been blind?

Ivy knew she had attended the party mostly because she wanted to spend time with Jacob and see if she had truly overlooked a decent man for all that time.

"You're David's mom, right?" A tall brunette asked and Ivy turned to her and nodded.

"Yes. Ivy Bontrager."

"Caylin Rogers. I'm Sofie's mom. Sofie talks about David all the time. I think she's a little in love with him."

Ivy tried to remember which one was Sofie. David made friends easily with his boyish charms and there was no shortage of boys and girls surrounding him.

"David speaks of her too," Ivy fibbed.

"These parties are so lame," Caylin sighed. "You'd think they'd spring for a keg of beer or a box of wine at least."

She grimaced.

"Sorry, you probably think I'm a heathen or something."

Ivy tensed at the woman's brash demeanor but she only smiled kindly.

"Of course not. I do not mind indulging in a glass of wine now and again."

"Oh, thank God," Caylin muttered. "The other parents swear you Amish are all wound tight but I knew it couldn't be that bad. After all, Jacob Morley is one of you and I think he's delicious!"

Inexplicably, Ivy felt a flash of anger, the words infuriating her more than they should have.

"Oh, speak of the devil," Caylin chirped. "Aw damn! He brought a date!"

Ivy spun, her skirt swirling at her ankles. Her mouth dropped open when she realized that Caylin was right. On Jacob's arm was Susanna Miller, beaming almost foolishly as Jacob escorted her into the banquet hall.

Envy coursed through Ivy's veins and when Jacob's eyes rested on hers, the expression on his face froze.

Of course he brought a date. Why would I expect him to come alone?

She thought of how he had tried to ask her to accompany him and she had brushed him off without a second thought.

And now I have waited too long and he has moved on with Susanna Miller.

It seemed impossible that he would have a change of heart so quickly but who could say what Jacob was feeling? After two years of trying to get her attention, she couldn't blame him for moving on.

"Oh, he's coming this way!" Caylin chortled and Ivy had officially decided she did not much care for the woman, mother of David's friend or not.

"Excuse me," Ivy mumbled, not wanting to be nearby when he approached. She was sure her humiliation was painted on her face and she didn't trust herself not to say something foolish.

"Where are you going? Can you grab me another cup of that god-awful punch if you're going that way?" the abrasive woman yelled after her but Ivy ignored her. She wasn't going that way. The only place she was headed was out the door and to her wagon.

It was not meant to be with Jacob and I, she thought, swallowing her misery and again, she wondered from where this newfound emotion had stemmed.

Last week you did not even know he cared about you and you had not given him the time of day.

Yet no amount of reasoning could shake the mounting sense of loss in Ivy's gut.

~ ~ ~

"Danke for inviting me to your function, Jacob. It was great fun to meet your Englisch friends," Susanna told him as he pulled the wagon before her house. "Would you care to come inside and say hello to my familye?"

He shook his head and peered at her in the dark, the outline of her face barely visible against the shadowy light of the moon.

"I have a long ride back to my home," he told her. "Send them my regards."

Even in the darkness, he saw her disappointment although she didn't speak it aloud and Jacob was once more left wondering what Matthew had told her about attending the party as his date. He had hoped that the deacon was forthcoming with her, that the outing was merely platonic but he had been given the impression throughout the night that Susanna had much more on her mind.

It bothered Jacob a great deal to think that Susanna had been misled but he was equally troubled that Ivy had left as soon as he had arrived. Jacob was left to wonder if she had been upset to see him with someone else but given the way she had ignored his earlier attempts to know her better, he couldn't reconcile how that could be.

I should never have agreed to bring Susanna with me, he thought but it was too late for regrets now.

"Will I see you at service on Sunday?" Susanna asked hopefully and Jacob swallowed before nodding.

"Ja, I will be there."

"Perhaps we can travel together?"

Jacob sighed heavily, knowing he needed to set the girl right before her affections escalated. It was cruel to give her false hope when he knew his heart belonged to Ivy.

"Susanna, I do not think that is a wise idea," he told her softly. "I asked you along to the party because..."

He trailed off, realizing he could not tell her the full truth. It would only add insult to injury.

"Because what?" she demanded, her voice changing as a note of suspicion crept into her tone. "Are you playing a game I do not understand?"

"Of course not!" Jacob replied defensively. "I thought you and I could have a good time as friends."

Susanna turned her head away and stared ahead, unspeaking.

"Susanna, I am not looking to be involved with anyone romantically," he continued, his words faltering at the lie. He wished to let her down easily but his conscience was bothering him.

"Gut'n owed, Jacob," Susanna said curtly, slipping from the bench and onto the dirt below. She did not turn to look at him and rushed toward the door so quickly, she was nearly a blur to his eyes. Jacob wondered if she was in tears and he hoped not.

Mein Gotte. How did I manage to make a worse mess of things? He wondered. The door all but slammed in Susanna's wake and Jacob exhaled a breath of air he hadn't realized he'd been holding before urging the horse away from the Miller farm.

On the way home, he considered what to do next. He knew for certain that he would never again enlist the aide of Matthew King for any matters related to the heart.

By the time he reached his family's property on the outskirts of the district, Jacob had decided there was only one thing he could do—avoid both Susanna and Ivy at all costs, no matter how difficult the latter might be to do.

I will keep our encounters minimal and short. I must forget about Ivy Bontrager and move on.

But even then, Jacob knew it would be easier said than done.

~ ~ ~

"Mammi are you ill?"

Ivy wasn't sure how to properly answer the question and she remained on her bed, staring up at the ceiling. She had been unable to leave the bedroom all morning, a strange weariness seeping into her bones which had started the moment she had seen Jacob with Susanna the previous night.

Iris had eyed her scornfully when she returned home so early.

"You cannot meet a suitor if you do not stay at the party," she chided Ivy reprovingly. "Sometimes I think you are happy cleaning toilets."

Ivy did not remind her mother-in-law that the land she rightfully owned had been hijacked. She was far too consumed with disappointment to engage in an argument with Iris. However, Iris' biting remarks did not help her mood in the least and a strange depression had sunk into Ivy's heart. Logically, she knew she was being foolish but that did nothing to alleviate the sadness she was feeling.

"Mammi?" Concern laced David's words and she forced herself to give him a comforting smile.

"Nee, liebling, I am merely thinking. Are you hungry?"

"Nee, I came to tell you that you have a caller."

Ivy bolted upright on the made bed, creasing the quilt beneath her. *Could it be Jacob?*

He had never come to her home before but she had no doubt he knew where she lived.

"Who is it?" she asked her son, the words emitting a squeak as she spoke.

"Gideon Byler."

Ivy blinked twice, the response making little sense in her own head.

"Who?" she asked, feeling dumkupp. Of course she knew who he was but that was the first thing to fall from her lips.

"Gideon Byler, the milk farmer?"

"Ja, ja," she mumbled, rising to her feet. "I remember. Wat is he doing here?"

"I don't know, Mammi. He did not say. Should I send him away?"

"Ja!"

The answer stunned her as it left her lips and David seemed uncomfortable at having to tell the man she was unavailable. Ivy had wanted nothing more than for Gideon to call upon her for a year and suddenly, she had no desire to see him whatsoever.

"What should I tell him?" David asked, lowering his voice as if he was afraid Gideon might overhear but Ivy was already brushing past her son to meet with the farmer. Despite her response, she knew she had to see what he wanted. She could not simply turn him away so rudely.

Even if I do not really wish to see him.

Ivy almost felt like she was dreaming as she made her way toward the front of the coach house where Gideon stood, seeming ill-at-ease as he waited for her. Ivy idly wondered if he had heard her response to his arrival.

"Hello Gideon," she said. "What brings you here?"

"Ivy." He nodded solemnly and Ivy glanced over her shoulder to where Gideon's eyes had travelled. David lurked behind the wall, the cuff of his pant leg visible.

"I was hoping that perhaps we could go for a walk today. I understand you do not work on the weekend."

Ivy's eyes narrowed curiously.

Has he been asking about me? Why is this the first I am learning about this?

"I am afraid I have no one to watch David but if he can come along, I would be happy to join you. Is something on your mind?"

Gideon face fell and Ivy's pulse quickened.

"I had hoped to speak to you privately," he muttered, casting David another look and Ivy realized how coldly he looked at her son.

Jacob never looks at David like that. He is always warm and caring around the children.

Suddenly Ivy realized that her son was likely the reason it had taken Gideon so long to approach her at all.

He does not care for children!

"As I said," she replied firmly. "I cannot leave him alone. He is only a boy of seven."

"He walks to the community center alone every day after school!" Gideon protested and Ivy saw that he knew much more about her than she ever expected. The understanding filled her with ire.

All this time I have been pining for this man and he has left me in limbo, wondering if I was good enough for him. All the while, he was simply biding his time, seeing if I was worthy of the effort.

Ivy's back became a steel rod and she threw her head back to stare at him defiantly.

"Gideon, I suspect whatever you have to say to me will be of no interest to me. We have chores to attend to here. If you don't mind..."

She stepped toward the door to see him through it and his mouth gaped.

"You are sending me away?" he asked dubiously. "Surely you must know that a widowed mother does not have many good options, Ivy. You may be lovely but you come with issues that most good men do not want."

He looked meaningfully at David and Ivy's face flushed.

"Get out!" she spat from between clenched teeth. "If you think yourself a good man, you are sorely mistaken."

She moved toward him, forcing him back over the threshold and slammed the door with finality in his wake.

"Mammi? Are you all right?" David whispered, running out to her side. His eyes were filled with tears. She had never been so angry with a man in her life.

"Ja, liebling. Do not worry. He is dumkupp. Do not listen to anything he has to say."

"Mammi, will you have a difficult time finding a husband because of me?"

"Nee! Gideon is wrong. There are many decent, good men who adore children and would be proud to call you their son."

She was thinking about one in particular. Slowly, Ivy exhaled and she imagined what would have happened if Gideon had called a week earlier. Would she have seen through his attractiveness in her love-hazed eyes?

She shuddered to think that she had almost fallen for the wrong man but Ivy quickly shoved the thought aside and turned to her son.

"Get a sweater, liebling. We are going out."

~ ~ ~

Eliza stuck her head into the barn where Jacob was applying a coat of lacquer upon a chair.

"Jake, you have a visitor," his teenaged sister told him and he looked up at her warily.

"It is not Susanna Miller, is it?" he breathed. All day he had expected retaliation from the slighted girl which was half the reason he had slunk into the barn that day—to remain hidden.

"Nee...it is Ivy Bontrager."

"Ivy?" He stood up so quickly, he knocked the lacquer can onto its side and Eliza giggled, turning away.

"Where is she?" Jacob called after her, righting the can.

"In the house. She has David with her."

Jacob paused at the revelation and chewed on the insides of his cheeks. It could not be a pleasant visit if she had brought her son, could it? Was she there to make a complaint? Withdraw David from the community center?

There was only one way to find out.

And I had hoped to avoid her for a few days, Jacob thought, sighing. He continued toward the house, wiping his hands on a soiled rag and found the pair in the front room.

"Jacob!" David called excitedly. His smile froze.

"I do not need to call you Mr. Morley outside the community center, do I?"

"Nee," Jacob laughed. "We are at home now. It is good to see you as always."

David's smile widened and Jacob nervously shifted his gaze toward the boy's mother.

"Hello, Ivy. I am sorry I did not get the opportunity to speak with you yesterday."

"I left early," she said quickly. "You had company."

Her cheeks flushed pink and Jacob realized instantly that she had been jealous of Susanna.

Matthew King may have been right after all.

"Susanna is just a friend," he heard himself say and he was sure his own cheeks were as rosy as Ivy's. He glanced warily at David.

"Would you care to join Eliza in the kitchen? She might be baking muffins," he suggested to the boy, sensing that the conversation was going to take a more adult tone but Ivy shook her head.

"Nee, I would like David here for this. He is what has inspired me to come," the blonde explained and Jacob nodded in agreement.

"Of course he can stay if you wish." Relief colored her expression and she cleared her throat slightly, settling her eyes on David's curious face.

"I have been very foolish," she commenced. Instantly, Jacob protested.

"Nee, you have not," he countered. "Whatever you believe you have done, you could never be foolish."

He meant his words sincerely. If he and Ivy never united, he still could not think badly of her.

"You are kind, Jacob and patient. I do not know why it took my son to show me your special qualities but if it was not for my son, I would not have realized that the most decent man in the district has been in front of me for two years."

Blood rushed through Jacob so quickly, he lost his breath and a surreal feeling overtook him. How long had he hoped to hear words like those from Ivy's full lips? How many nights had he stayed awake, envisioning her professing her feelings for him.

It is happening and I feel like I am in a dream!

Jacob had not realized that a deep silence had fallen until Ivy rushed on, her gaze fixed on the rug in the front room.

"I understand if I have missed my opportunity with you," she breathed. "I do not fault you for—"

"You have missed nothing!" he interrupted. "I could not let go of you if I tried."

He looked at David apologetically that someone so young should hear such mature words but the boy was beaming happily.

"You mean it?" Ivy gasped. "You would consider dating me?"

"I would be the fool if I said no," he replied. Their eyes locked over the dark blonde head of Ivy's son and the urge to kiss her overwhelmed Jacob.

"Perhaps it is a good idea for you to see Eliza now," Ivy murmured to David. The boy did not need to be told a second time and in seconds, Jacob had gathered Ivy into his arm and placed a sweet, long kiss upon her mouth.

It was well worth the excruciating wait.

BE GOOD, MY STARLIGHT : AN AMISH ROMANCE

NATALIE SALEM

Chapter One

"Be good, my starlight, I love you," Naomi said gently. She leaned down and hugged her son tight. He was just barely five, but was now old enough to start classes.

His golden hair looked nothing like her brown locks, his brown eyes were so dark compared to her green ones. He was hers, though, despite appearances. He was her entire world, and she knew that she'd do anything to make sure he was happy and unaware of the hardships she faced. He kissed her cheek, and then immediately ran off with a couple other boys to start their lessons.

Her family was setting her up with a stranger.

He was supposedly a good man.

Naomi was yet to see that, she knew that he'd be at her home with her family by the time she returned from her son's school. She knew he was a hard worker, that he had a daughter, and that he was ten years older than her.

She wasn't keen on him being thirty, but she knew that, given her circumstances, he was starting to look like the only option.

Naomi looked back at the school house as she started back home. The elderly teacher, Mister Lapp, was ushering in the last of the children, and she watched him with interest.

He had a job in this community.

A place.

Nobody would look at him and wonder why he was alone, or who he was.

She wished for a life so easy.

The soft summer grass gave way under her shoes as she headed back to the main street. Golden light, radiating off a bright morning sun, brought her entire village to life and motion around her.

Everyone was pleased to greet one another, everyone was starting their day and jobs.

Except her.

Nobody greeted her as she walked through the village, she kept her eyes averted in fear of any stray staring. She felt like how she imagined English must feel when they come into town with their shiny cars.

Different.

Unwanted.

She tried to distract herself, and remind herself of things she knew of Vernon.

He was 30, owned land as a farmer, was a widower. He had a daughter who was nearing seven and was in desperate need of a mother since she'd be out of school within the next handful of years.

Vernon sounded respectable.

Sounded like her only chance.

Still, as Naomi reached her family's home, she couldn't help but feel a pang of regret. A marriage without love wasn't much of a marriage. A marriage of convenience would help her family, help her reputation, help her life, but she'd still hurt. She'd still feel out of place and unhappy. She was sure of it. Naomi let herself in, pulled off her black bonnet, and reassured herself that this would be fine: she needed to think of her family and son first.

"Naomi, are you home?" her father called from the kitchen. She could smell that her mother was cooking something, despite the fact that they all just had breakfast.

"I am, father," she replied, following his voice. The kitchen was large, but as she walked in, and felt all eyes upon her, it felt very tight and small.

A man she'd never seen before was standing in the corner sipping what smelled like very dark coffee. He was taller than her, his face shaven to show he was unmarried. She noted that he was handsome, that he looked sturdy and strong, but she felt no strong pull to him.

"This is Vernon Miller," her father introduced, motioning to the man. "We were talking about the idea of marriage between you two," he said flatly.

Naomi felt her heart drop.

She knew that this was her family's goal, but she'd thought she'd been given the chance to court first. She looked to her mother for help, but her mother just cast her eyes aside and turned back to cooking.

"It's good to meet you," Vernon said, standing and offering his hand to her. The action felt incredibly intimate, given what was just said, but she took his hand and shook it softly anyways. His grip was firm, his hand was warm.

She didn't want this.

Still, she knew better than to be rude.

"Nice to meet you as well," she replied.

"Can I drive you home from church on Sunday?" he offered. Naomi almost laughed, that was the kind of courting only teenagers did, and he was almost twice the age he should be to ask.

Her father gave her a stern look, though.

"I would like that," she replied. "Would you like more coffee?"

"I would be very thankful for more," he answered, not taking his eyes off of hers. A blush flooded her cheeks from the attention, and Naomi quickly took his mug to get out of his sight.

He talked with her father comfortably about the farm work, about how much land he owned. It discomforted her to realize he was the same space in age from her parents as he was to her. She couldn't imagine her mother or father marrying someone so much younger than they were.

Naomi gave him his coffee, and he stopped to spare her a smile before he continued talking. He was trying harder to impress her parents than he was to impress her, she didn't mind. She was almost complemented to think that he actually wanted her.

Soon he was leaving, and she was set to work in the garden to keep it weeded and watered.

She was sure if she set her mind to it she could love him.

She was 20, the age most girls would be able to choose if they wanted to leave the church or not. The age most women would have dozens of offers and freedom to choose as they wished.

Yet she had to scramble and grab to get the one offer she did.

Her family loved her, cared about her, and they were trying to make sure that she lived happily. They didn't want to see her grow old and alone, with just her son in her life.

They didn't want her to have to spend her entire life in their home.

A plane passed overhead, and Naomi craned her neck and let herself watch it. She couldn't help but wonder, if her situation had been different and she were English instead, would she have been happier with that life?

She'd had the choice taken from her, though.

Naomi had sworn to the church and was going to live her whole life happily being a part of it.

She loved her son, John, would do anything to protect him and raise him well. She'd fallen pregnant with him at just fifteen.

Fallen from grace in the community when she gave birth to him at age fifteen.

She'd had many friends, had a fun life, before her pregnancy.

She'd gone to sings to meet boys, had been courted by two, and yet one poor decision had left her ostracized from everyone but family.

Sighing as the plane went out of sight, Naomi felt resigned.

She'd make herself fall in love with him.

Almost six years since she was found to be pregnant had passed, almost six years she had spent unwanted.

He wanted her.

He was interested in her.

She couldn't see herself getting another chance like this, and she didn't want to let down her family.

She'd love him eventually, she was sure of it.

Chapter Two

The next day, a bright and sunny Tuesday, Naomi and her son arrived to the school to find it closed. A sign hung on the door, white crisp paper with clear handwriting. When she could finally get close enough, through the gaggle of mothers and children reading it, she was shocked.

Mister Lapp, the elderly school teacher, had passed in the night from a heart attack.

Naomi walked John home, disturbed and unsure of how to explain it to him. He didn't have to deal with death yet, her parents, and her parent's parents, were all alive still.

She hadn't expected him to pass, then again she never really saw death coming for anyone. Once someone got to a certain age they moved back in with one of their children to live out their retirement in comfort. Most people didn't work until they died.

The rest of her day was spent more heavily considering marrying Vernon. If she passed he would be much more able to take care of her son than her aging parents or her two older siblings who had left the church.

The next day, despite her heart telling her the school would still be closed, she walked her son the same path she did most days.

Nobody else with children were about, nobody seemed to be heading to the school. She felt foolish at first, before realizing someone was in the school house.

The sign was gone from the door.

"Hello?" she asked, holding her son's hand as she peeked inside the schoolhouse doors. There was a young man at the front of the classroom, flipping through a book. He looked up at the sound of her voice and smiled.

"Hello! Please, come in," he said, motioning to her and John. She couldn't help but notice the rest of the room was empty besides them, usually there were at least twenty children in class every day.

"Where is everyone?" she asked, surprised.

"I was just asking myself the same question," he smiled sadly, looking pointedly around. "They may be taking a day to grieve," he offered as an explanation.

"Must be," she murmured, trying not to notice how handsome the man was. He had a strong jawline, but sweet blue eyes. His cheekbones were sharp, and they led her attention to his soft looking lips. His face was clean shaven. Unmarried.

His looks were hard to ignore.

"I'll call it an off day, then," he sighed, leaning back against his desk.

"Are you from the area?" she found herself asking. She was sure she'd know if she'd seen him before. He was too attractive to be forgettable, and too close-looking to her age for him to have not been to the same sings and gatherings as her.

"I've been caught," he joked. He was lighthearted, warm. She was caught off guard and found herself savoring it. Not many people in her village even acted like she existed anymore. Years of shame had left her starving for any kind of positive attention. "I'm from a town in Idaho, I wanted a move to see what the rest of our churches had to offer," he explained.

"Have you taught before?"

"Mommy can we go?" her son interrupted before the new man could answer.

"John, I need you to have patience," she said softly, leaning down to his height. He looked slightly scolded, but sat down in one of the chairs and waited.

"He's so well behaved," the new teacher said, watching him.

"Thank you," she said gently. A child who misbehaved was a bad mark on the parent and she knew it. A compliment on her son was a compliment to her.

"Of course," he replied. "I'm Eli," he walked towards her, offering his hand.

"Naomi," she said softly, accepting his hand and shaking it. She felt shocks go through her body at the contact. What was this feeling?

He let go of her hand slowly, and she immediately missed the contact.

"I taught grades kindergarten through third for a year in Idaho," he said, answering the question she'd asked earlier.

"I see," Naomi made herself answer.

She wanted to say more, to ask more, but she forced herself to have some control.

"We should go," she said after a moment, looking down at her son who was starting to drift off to sleep. "Thank you, I'll make sure word gets out that there will be class tomorrow," she said gently, smiling.

"That would be very kind," he smiled. "Have a good day," he offered.

"You also," she nodded, leading her son out.

She'd found him attractive.

More than that, she corrected herself, she was attracted to him.

Quietly she admonished herself as they headed back to her parent's home. She knew better than to seek the attention of men. She knew that it never worked out well for her.

Yet she found herself glancing back at the schoolhouse to see if she could catch a glimpse of the new teacher.

He was looking out the window back at them.

Color fled onto her cheeks and she looked back towards their path. He was handsome, educated. He had a job that would leave him being an important part of the community.

Eli.

She repeated his name in her mind.

It was a common name, but it felt special attached to him. She regretted not learning his last name, and as she had this thought more guilt fled her heart.

If he knew anything about her.

About her situation.

He wouldn't have been so sweet to her, she was sure of it.

Eli was kind because he was a teacher, because it was his job to be, not because he was interested in her. She took a deep breath and reminded herself that her family had picked a very suitable man for her anyways.

This was just cold feet.

Her family had laid a very straight line for her, and if she followed it she could be very happy.

Vernon was an older man, but he had lived there his whole life, had roots in the community. Eli was attractive and closer to her age, but he would want to start from scratch with a respectable wife.

Not with her.

Naomi scooped up her son and carried him the rest of the way home in her arms, trying not to admit to herself how excited she was to see Eli the next day.

Chapter Three

The next morning there were many people at the school.

Eli was talking, and smiling, and being more than friendly with the other mothers who had come. Naomi took it as confirmation that he really was just being nice to her.

She didn't need to read into him too much.

Tightening her bonnet a little she walked John the rest of the way to the school.

"Miss Naomi," he greeted her, his smile warm and welcoming.

"I don't think I caught your last name," she replied, also smiling.

"Troyer," he answered, a friendly sound in his voice.

"Do take care of my boy, Mister Troyer," she said softly.

"He won't be too much trouble," Eli replied, shaking his head and smiling.

Naomi spent the rest of the walk home memorizing his smile.

That evening she got to thank him for his care, again.

His face stayed in her mind.

"You're smiling a lot today," he mother commented, the water on the stove started to boil. "Is it that you're keen to the idea of Mister Miller now?" she asked. There were no notes of teasing in her voice, it was an honest question.

"I'm keen to the idea of marriage," Naomi replied, keeping her answer vague.

She didn't want her mother to know.

The next day was Friday.

She tried to make excuses for herself as to why they were arriving at the school house a full twenty minutes later. The warm muffins in her basket were enough evidence to prove them all wrong.

"Mister Troyer?" she knocked on the schoolhouse door and peeked in. He was looking through papers at his desk. At their intrusion he glanced at the wind-up clock on his desk.

"You're early," he said, it wasn't accusing or confused, he was almost pleased sounding.

"I thought I'd welcome you properly to the community," she offered, bringing forward the muffins.

"They smell very good, thank you," he said, standing to meet them halfway to the door.

"Sorry about being so early, I was up early this morning and lost track of my time," she apologized as he accepted the basket.

"No, please, you're fine," he replied, shaking his head. "I haven't eaten today and these are a welcome sight," he added.

She went home that day feeling like she was floating.

Friday turned into Saturday, and then soon it was Sunday and Vernon was greeting her at church.

She'd almost forgotten about him.

Now, after she'd spent so many days getting glimpses and small moments with Eli at the schoolhouse, Vernon seemed very different to her.

He was older, more of a man. She knew thirty wasn't old by any standards, but Eli was her age. Vernon seemed more stern suddenly, and less interesting. He nodded to her, cordially, properly, and then she sat with her family.

The service was a memorial to Mister Lappe, the school teacher.

Guilt flooded Naomi again, it was her norm. She'd not mourned the teacher, she was too busy being interested in the new one.

In Eli.

In her interest and attraction, she'd lost her morals.

Naomi bowed her head, listening to the sermon, and started to pray for forgiveness. Regardless of how lonely she'd been, she didn't need to become selfish and thoughtless.

Vernon was an actual choice.

Her only choice.

Whatever she was thinking was interest from Eli was nothing more than courtesy from a teacher to his student's parent. She knew this, she needed to keep it in mind. If he knew anything about her, if he had the slightest inkling about how the town viewed her, he wouldn't be so friendly.

Flirting towards him, paying him any attention, was empty and useless.

She needed to get that through her head.

Newly resigned, she sat through the rest of the service and listened carefully. When church finally wound down to an end her family left her behind without mention, leading a sleepy John away for a nap. Naomi wished she could go with them and not have to talk to Vernon.

He appeared to her through the crowd, a small smile on his mouth, and she followed him to his buggy. Vernon was thoughtful, helping her up into the buggy, carrying on comfortable conversation about her family and his work.

He was sweet.

It made it worse.

She couldn't help but feel like if he were rude, if there was anything about him that she didn't like, she'd have an out.

He gave her no excuses.

He was kind, gentle, understanding. He was everything that, before knowing Eli, she would have wanted in a man. Her family had a keen eye in choosing him to be introduced to her, and she appreciated that. She wished he held her interest as well as Eli had.

"Your mother invited me for dinner Tuesday night," he said idly as they neared her home. "I wanted to check that you also want me there," he added, turning to her.

"We would all love to have you there," she said, not meaning it.

Her parents would love to have him there, and she would love to make her parents happy, regardless of what that meant for her.

Chapter Four

Monday came and Naomi didn't pause to greet Eli. She didn't make eye contact with him or smile to him as she dropped off her son.

She'd convinced herself that if she was going to rid herself of affection for him, the best way to do it was to stop letting herself talk warmly to him. Any interaction would be too much, and she wouldn't let it happen.

At least, she thought she wouldn't.

Six hours later, when she returned to pick up John, Eli asked her to stay after the class cleared out. She agreed to, feeling her heart race as he said her name. She beat down the feelings, but they just simmered under the surface instead. Her traitorous heart didn't care about what was right or pure, it just wanted his attention.

"Has John done something wrong?" she asked as the last of the children left with their mothers.

"No, never, he's a model student," Eli replied, shaking his head. He gathered the papers his students had left behind from their desks. "May I step outside with you while he stays in here?" Eli asked, making eye contact with her. His expression was apologetic, and her heart warmed over it.

She adored him.

"Did I anger you?" he asked as they stepped out. The day was overcast, the strong winds above pushed the clouds at an alarmingly high speed. There would be a storm by morning.

"No," she was honest.

"Are you well?" he asked, he was obviously concerned. She needed to clear the air or it would torture her forever. If she just leapt to Vernon's side as his wife without ever knowing if there was a chance with Eli, she'd never forgive herself.

"Why do you pay me attention?" she asked, the words tumbled out of her mouth like heavy stones.

He looked taken aback for just a moment. "I find you interesting, you're very kind and I want to return the favor," he answered.

"Nothing more?" she asked, unsure. His expression faltered for a moment.

"That's not entirely true," he sighed, leaning against the schoolhouse. He glanced in to look at John for a moment. "I find my thoughts stay with you even when you're not here," he admitted. "At first, I pushed it aside because I assumed you were married because of John," he said. "One of the other mothers mentioned you were single and lived with your parents, so I felt no guilt in talking to you."

"Even with a child out of wedlock?" she asked.

He looked uneasy for a moment. "It's something I would have to heavily consider before courting you."

"You'd consider courting me?" Naomi was even more surprised by this bit of information.

"I would at some point," he said, honestly. She read it as a 'no' since it wasn't a 'yes.

"I don't mean to make you uncomfortable," she replied, her heart dropping into her stomach. "I just," she sighed. "I misunderstood your intentions and I'm terribly sorry."

"Don't be," Eli said, shaking his head. "I'm not sure what I feel for you, I need to reflect and pray on it, can you give me a week?" he asked, his eyes were warm and sweet.

"Of course, take your time," Naomi answered, as if she weren't being rushed to marry Vernon.

She gathered John and they left.

John was happy to talk about how much he enjoyed Eli's lessons better, that they were more interesting than how Mister Lapp had taught them. Naomi scolded him for speaking ill of someone, if if they're dead, but was pleased to know her son took a shining to Eli. He hadn't even shown a little bit of interest in Vernon.

Tuesday morning when she took her son to school, she didn't talk to Eli or make eye contact with him. It was the same when she picked her son up after.

She didn't want to seem like she was trying to seduce him, didn't want to sway Eli into something he didn't want.

That night, Vernon was at their home for dinner. He and her father spoke about the weather, and of crops for the year. Naomi tried to pay attention and be as sweet and appealing as possible.

He could never know that she was on the verge of crying because of another man. It would just add more shame to who she was. Her mother stopped before cleaning dishes to invite him for dinner on Friday as well, and he accepted.

Her parents were getting her further and further into this man's life.

What would happen if by some miracle Eli accepted her and they started courting? Would her parents hate her for yanking them around?

Would they ever forgive her?

Nightfall found her sobbing in the garden after she set John to bed. Crickets filled the air with their noise, and she tried to distract herself with them.

She's only fallen pregnant with John because she'd kept secrets from her parents. She fell in love with a boy, and he tried to introduce her to all that he knew of the English. How wild and adventurous their lives could be, how different it was from their own world.

Naomi became swept up in those ideas.

She went further with him, becoming intimate, not entirely knowing what she was doing. Her mother had only ever said, "never take your dress off around anyone else,".

She fell pregnant.

Then, during the boy's Rumspringa, he'd left.

Left the church, left his family, left her.

Her parents were furious, they had expected him to marry her and be forced into staying with the church- but they couldn't take that choice away from him.

He left.

She never got to fully enjoy her Rumspringa because of him.

Never got to finish being young.

She was forced immediately into motherhood, into following that path, before she even got to see the world outside of her community. The people around her looked down on her for being a single mother so young, she felt every glare and sneer that had struck her over the last five years. Her shame was too painful.

All of this because she kept a secret from her parents.

Naomi wiped her face, but the tears kept falling.

"Naomi, what is it?" her mother's soft voice said from behind. Naomi jumped a little, startled, but then began to cry more at the sight of her.

"I think I love another man, mother," she explained. "He's considering courting me, and asked a week to think it over," she confessed it quickly, the words poured out of her like water.

"Why didn't you tell me?" her mother asked, sitting beside her she wrapped her arm around Naomi.

"I'm worried I'm being selfish again," she answered. Her mother didn't respond immediately, just sat their and held her softly.

"He sounds like a thoughtful man for waiting to think about it, and you sound like you've been thinking it over too," her mother answered. "I'll ask your father to tell Mister Miller to come next week instead of Friday, and if this other man asks to court you, we'll consider him instead," she explained.

"Are you sure?" Naomi asked, wiping her face.

"We just want you to be married and happy like we are, that's all," her mother explained.

"Thank you," Naomi sighed, ready and hopeful for Eli to give her an answer.

The rest of the week slid by like thick tar.

She tried to avoid looking at him at all, but kept catching her eyes flicking over to him and watching him. She wasn't happy that she had to see him twice a day, and started dreading taking John to and from school. Every time she saw Eli and he didn't approach her with an answer it felt like a more definite 'no'.

Sunday came, and he'd still not said anything.

Vernon offered to drive her home, and she let him, but she didn't say a word the whole way home. He didn't seem to notice. Unlike Eli, who immediately pointed out that she was acting odd, Vernon just kept talking about how he wanted to raise a new barn.

She was exhausted of him, and was starting to loathe how secure he seemed in marrying her.

***

Finally, it was Monday morning.

She wore her black bonnet, and her favorite dress and cape.

It wasn't flashy. Nothing she, or anyone around her, wore was, but it was her favorite shade of blue, and she felt lovely in it. She left early with John, so that Eli wouldn't have to say anything in front of anyone, and tried to keep a lid on her energy.

When she arrived he was behind his desk, writing.

"Sorry we're early, is it alright if I leave him here?" she asked. These were the first words she'd said to him in a week.

"That's fine," he answered, barely looking up from his papers.

It was a no, then.

Naomi nodded, then turned and bit her lip as she started to walk home. He didn't want to court her. Eli had no interest in her. Her heart ached, and she tried to remind herself that she still had Vernon as a possibility, she wouldn't be alone.

Somehow, that made it worse.

Chapter Five

She didn't tell her mother his answer when she got home.

She didn't start the laundry, like she did every Monday. She didn't do anything but go to her room and kneel to pray.

Naomi wanted answers.

She needed to know what to do next, where to take her path. Should she just give up on any other men and marry Vernon now that he was the only choice? Should she stay single and hope another eventually notices her?

Both options sounded terrible, but they were her only two.

The way he didn't even look her in the face burned at her heart again, and she started praying harder, looking for guidance between her tears. She didn't want to be alone for the rest of her life, but she also didn't want to end up in a loveless marriage. Her week of talking to and falling for Eli had been so warm and good, and although it was short lived she wanted to feel that way more. She wanted to feel loved.

Her mother came in to gather the sheets, starting the laundry since Naomi hadn't yet, and paused for a moment.

"It's been a week, today, and I think his answer is 'no,'" Naomi explained, standing up from kneeling.

"Then it's a blessing you also have Vernon in your life," her mother said, patting Naomi's hair softly for a moment, like she did when her daughter was younger. "We love you and will be here for you for as long as you want us," her mother explained.

Naomi knew that wouldn't last forever.

Her mother would need to retire eventually, would need someone to take care of her and offer her a home. Both of Naomi's older siblings left the church and wouldn't be able to offer that. If Naomi stayed single there was no way she could support them.

She'd have to marry Vernon. Marrying him was the only way to be sure that she could properly thank them for all they'd done for her. The only way to show God, and the church, that she truly was thankful for all she had.

"Tomorrow I'll tell father I'll marry Vernon if he'll have me. Today my heart needs to mourn," Naomi said, hugging her mother close.

"We're proud of you Naomi," her mother said. "We love you and John, we're glad to have you in our home," she explained.

Naomi cleaned her face and then set to helping with the laundry, letting it distract her.

The day passed more quickly now, and she almost lost track of the time. An hour before she was supposed to leave to pick John up from school, her son came running out to the garden to her.

"John! What are you doing here?" she asked, alarmed.

"Mister Troyer let us out early," he answered, hugging against her leg.

"Who walked you home?" she leaned down and looked him over, ensuring he was fine. His golden hair was so much like Eli's that she could almost see him as his son.

"Mister Troyer," he answered. "He told all the others that it was a short day," he went on. Then John began to babble about a math problem he was able to solve, but Naomi was completely distracted.

Why hadn't he told her it was a short day?

Why did he walk her son home?

Naomi stood quickly, looking over her dress and making sure that the soap hadn't soaked it. Taking John's hand in hers, she headed back into her parent's home.

There were voices in the main room of the house, and she followed through the kitchen to them.

Eli was sitting on a couch opposite her parents, and was talking to them comfortably. Naomi's heart was beating out of her chest, suddenly and strong.

He was here.

He was here and smiling at her.

She smiled back chastely, remembering herself, and sat down beside her mother. John kissed her goodbye and ran off to his room to do his homework.

"I want to court your daughter," Eli said flatly. "I know that usually this is done in other ways, that it would be kept quietly, but I learned this last week that Vernon was wanting her hand, and so I don't have the option to stay quiet." He watched over her parents carefully. The words caught Naomi by surprise and her whole body felt like it was buzzing.

He wanted to court her! She'd been resigned to being stuck marrying Vernon for her parent's future security, and now here was Eli. She knew she could so easily love him, she was already most of the way there, and they'd be happy together.

Naomi's mother exchanged a look with her, as if confirming this was the man she had cried over. When Naomi nodded, her mother turned to Naomi's father and murmured something softly to him.

His demeanor changed just slightly into a softer one.

"Do you own land?" her father asked, sitting back in his seat.

"I do, it has a home on it and room for a garden," Eli replied.

"Would your end intent be marriage?" her father asked. Naomi's heart pounded at the question.

"It would be," Eli didn't hesitate in saying his.

Naomi's heart was soaring. She tried to remember what prayers she had said before so that she could thank God for answering each of them. She wanted so much to just walk across the room and kiss Eli and say that she wanted the same.

The room was quiet, though.

She began to realize it had been a couple minutes since Eli answered, and her father still hadn't said anything. She turned to look at her father, gray seeping into his once-red beard, and watched his expression. He looked like he was seriously considering things.

"I see no problem in it," her father answered finally, breathing out slowly. "Just be true to her," he added.

"I will be," Eli replied.

He stayed a little longer and spoke casually with her father, looking over to Naomi every few moments like she was made of the stars themselves.

Nightfall began to near, and her mother offered for him to stay for dinner, but he declined and said he had to go over the tests.

"Naomi will walk you out then," her father said, heading to the kitchen with his wife.

Naomi's cheeks colored at the idea that her parents were leaving them alone. They stood together and headed to the front door slowly, their arms brushing.

"I'm sorry I didn't talk to you properly this morning," he said as they walked. "I was nervous to say it, to let it out, but I needed your family's permission first," he explained. "If I had spoken to you for more than a second I would have asked you to court me," he said, he was almost laughing.

"I'm so pleased you want to court me," it felt like an understatement, but she had to say something. "I like you very much," she admitted. They stood there, comfortable in each others silence, for a couple minutes as the evening's crickets began to pick up.

"I look forward to seeing you in the morning," he said gently, turning to her. "I always do," a smile was on his mouth.

"I do also," she replied.

He leaned towards her, and she met him halfway.

The kiss was gentle and sweet. His lips sent sparks through hers and in that moment she could see their future together.

A marriage with love.

Everything she'd ever wanted.

END

KAYLA

44

MONICA MARKS

It was Kayla's favorite time of year and when she woke that morning, she inhaled deeply, absorbing the nostalgic feeling which the onset of autumn brought along.

It is time for harvest and engagement announcements, she thought happily, swinging her long legs off the single mattress and scurrying to the window to stare into to endless farmland. The smallest frost had settled overnight but there was no cause for concern; the sunshine was fighting to warm the October day already and it was just past dawn. She tried to ignore the near exhaustion in her bones and stretched, willing herself to wake up.

I slept more than enough, she reasoned with her weary body. *There is no reason for me to be so tired.*

She told herself that the crisp fall air would invigorate her.

"Kayla!"

Her younger sister, Hannah threw open the door to her bedroom and folded her small arms across her chest.

"Haven't you dressed yet? It is almost seven o'clock!"

"Haven't you learned to knock yet? You are almost eight years old," Kayla replied haughtily. The sisters stared at each other before bursting into laughter.

"I am coming, Hannah," she assured the child. "There is time for breakfast and to walk to school."

Hannah smiled and Kayla clapped her hands.

"You lost another tooth!" she declared, rushing forward to examine her sister's mouth. "Let me see."

Hannah opened her mouth obligingly and the older sister patted her cheek.

"Go show *Daed* now," she instructed. "I will be along in a moment."

Hannah turned to leave Kayla, rushing down the steps toward the kitchen and Kayla hurried to change.

Hannah was not wrong; she had slept in again. It seemed to be happening with more frequency and Kayla had first believed the change of weather had been affecting her but suddenly she was not so certain.

I must eat better, she chided herself, slipping into a dark brown work dress and fastening an apron atop her skirt. *Autumn is not the time to waste time sleeping when Daed needs help with harvest and winter preparations. If you are so tired when the days are still long, what will you be like in two months?*

She padded across the threshold and into the corridor, trying to recall what needed to be done that morning. Canning needed to be started, the hay baled, pickling, jams...the list was endless as always and Kayla began to form a list in her mind in order of importance.

Slipping down the stairs, Kayla was suddenly overwhelmed by a wave of dizziness. She clutched the bannister, blood draining from her face as she tried to gather her bearings.

Oh Gotte, I do not have the luxury of being sick, she warned herself, willing a feeling of normalcy to come but in seconds, her legs had buckled and to her horror, Kayla tumbled down the remaining three steps onto the landing.

Not again! She thought, horrified, knowing that her family would witness her embarrassment this time. It was the third fainting spell she had experienced in two weeks but gratefully, her father and sister had not seen the others.

As spots of black and red danced before her eyes, she opened her mouth to moan but she began to lose consciousness as Hannah came running into the foyer, their father in tow.

The last thing she recalled before the world went dark was her small sister screaming.

When she woke, Jeremiah Roth stood praying over her, his eyes closed but even without reading the expression in his gentle blue irises, Kayla could see the concern in his face.

"*Daed*?" she called weakly, struggling to sit up against the bed. She realized she had been put back in her room, tucked in snugly among blankets.

"Oh, Kayla!" Jeremiah gasped, his lids flying open at the sound of her voice. "You must remain still. I have asked the Fishers to call for Dr. Imhoff."

"I am fine, *Daed*," Kayla protested. "It was nothing, I am sure. It happens sometimes."

"How many times?" Jeremiah demanded, his cornflower blue eyes wide with shock. "Why did you not tell me before?"

"It is no cause for alarm. Cancel the doctor!" Kayla groaned.

"Hush, *liebchen*," he insisted, pointing at the bed. "You will remain here until the doctor has seen you."

"We haven't time for this," Kayla insisted, attempting to rise again. "We have much to do."

"I am your father," Jeremiah growled with uncharacteristic sternness. "You will do as you are told. The harvest can wait."

Kayla settled back, blinking.

"All right, *Daed*," she relented. "I will wait but the Dr. Imhoff will tell you there is nothing wrong."

"I would rather hear it from him," Jeremiah replied. "He is the one with the medical degree after all."

He turned to the bedside and produced a glass of water.

"Drink this. I will wait downstairs Jonah."

"Where is Hannah?"

"Lydia Fisher has taken her to school. You mustn't worry, Kayla. All is tended to this morning. Your job is to rest."

He turned to leave the room before Kayla could form another argument, leaving her to stare at the ceiling is mild exasperation.

This is foolish, she thought but she dared not express her feelings aloud. She knew her father was concerned and she had no one to blame but herself.

I have been neglecting meals and sleeping poorly, she chided herself. *Now I have worried everyone.*

In minutes, she heard footfalls on the stairs and the door opened.

"*Guter mayire*, Kayla," Dr. Imhoff announced, smiling in his kindly way. "I understand you had a small fainting episode this morning."

Kayla stifled a sigh.

"It was nothing," she insisted.

"I will see about that," Jonah Imhoff replied lightly, opening his bag.

He checked her eyes and throat, running her temperature and pinching her skin to test for validity.

Then he turned to Jeremiah.

"We will talk outside," he told the patriarch, patting Kayla's face warmly.

"You should rest today, Kayla," he told her, closing his bag. Kayla chewed on her tongue to keep a thousand objections from erupting and watched helplessly as the men retreated into the hallway.

She strained her ears to listen, catching only a few words as she did.

"...tests...color...must be vigilant."

Their voices cut in and out but Kayla felt a prickle slide down her back as she understood the gist of their conversation.

He believes there is something wrong with me, she realized, concern floating through her for the first time since the incidents had begun. She tried to dismiss the feeling of worry but when her father returned to the bedroom, his eyes shone with something she had not seen in many years.

"Jonah is arranging for you to have tests done at Lancaster General Hospital," he told her gravely. Kayla swallowed quickly, realizing there was a lump in her throat.

"What does he believe is wrong, *Daed*?" she whispered and Jeremiah seemed to recognize his mistake, wiping the dismayed frown from his face.

"Nothing specific, *liebchen*," he replied quickly. "It is merely a precaution. Do not fret; we will learn what ails you soon enough."

"*Daed,* I am certain it is - "

"You are not a doctor, Kayla. In the meanwhile, you will rest. I will see if Lydia can stay with you while I tend to the farm," he continued and Kayla heard no room for debate in his tone.

"*Daed*, you cannot tend the farm alone," she sighed. "You would better have Lydia help you."

Jeremiah stared at her for a long while as if he was looking directly through her.

"You are correct," he told her softly. "I must enlist help until you are better."

Without another word, he spun and walked from the bedroom, leaving Kayla to stare after him with her mouth agape in question.

The wagon drew near the farmhouse, Lydia Fisher leading the horse through the grey day. They were returning from Kayla's appointment at the hospital where she had undergone bloodwork for her ever increasing fainting and general fatigue.

"Would you like me to come with you, Kayla?" Lydia asked as she slid from the bench onto the dirt. Kayla stifled a sigh and shook her head, forcing a smile onto her lips. She was growing tired of being coddled by both her father and the neighbors, despite their good intentions.

"I feel fine," she fibbed. In reality, she wished to lay down but she dared not say anything to Lydia. The last thing she wished to do was cause more of a fuss.

"I will be by later this evening to fix supper for you," Lydia told her, picking up the reins. "Back to bed now."

Kayla did not answer but waved at the butcher's wife as she made her way from the Roth farm toward her own.

I will go mad if I have to spend one more minute in bed, Kayla thought glumly, turning toward the fields. She saw her father in the distance, reaping corn and she longed to run toward him but she did not. She would only interrupt him and take more time from his duties.

Duties I should be tending to also, she told herself, guilt wracking her body.

The doctor at the hospital had been candid with her assessment, citing several reasons for her strange illness.

"But we will run the necessary tests, Kayla and determine the cause."

It was not until Kayla and Lydia were almost home that she realized that the physician had told her nothing of sustenance.

I can only wait for the results – however long that will take. In the meanwhile, Daed is working alone on the farm.

Suddenly, another figure appeared, close to the entrance of the maize and Kayla started.

"Hello!" she called out, her brow furrowing with concern. The stranger turned to look at her and he seemed to freeze as they stared at one another.

"Hello," he replied, turning to face her. Kayla stepped back in surprise as he emerged from the stalks, dressed in pair of blue jeans and a black and red flannel shirt.

"Who are you?" she demanded as she stared at him uncomprehendingly. "Does my father know you are here?"

The dark-haired man paused, cocking his head to the side slightly, a single strand of hair falling directly onto his forehead.

"Yes," he answered. "My name is Will. Will Jenkins."

Kayla waited for him to elaborate on why he stood on their land but he did not speak. Slowly, she drew closer to him.

"Why are you on our land?" Kayla asked, her green eyes narrowing in suspicion. She loathed that she was immediately concerned about the Englisher's presence but she could not reconcile one good reason that the man would be on the property.

"I am helping with the harvest," Will told her simply.

"Helping whom?"

Will stared at her for a long moment as if he was concerned she was slow-witted.

"I am helping the owner of the land obviously," he replied dryly. "Who are you?"

Kayla was reluctant to disclose any information to the man, her eyes lifting to see where her father was in the field.

Daed wouldn't hire an Englisher to help on the farm, she thought, distrustful of Will Jenkins. *And he certainly did not mention bringing on any help.*

To her relief, she was Jeremiah approaching.

"There is my father now," Kayla said sternly. "If you do not belong here, you best run along before he catches you on our property."

Will gave her a bemused smile.

"If I ran along, I would not be doing my job," he told her lightly. "I think your father would be angrier at that."

"Kayla you are home," Jeremiah cried, hurrying toward his daughter. She watched as he glanced nervously at the stranger.

"Come inside and we will talk," the senior Roth said, without acknowledging the Englisher in their midst. Kayla opened her mouth to speak but the look in her father's eye silenced her.

"Yes, *Daed,*" she agreed, turning to follow Jeremiah inside the house. Will remained in place, his mouth upturned and Kayla cast him one long look before entering the house.

"Daed, did you hire that Englisher to help with the harvest?" she asked dubiously.

"Yes, but that is unimportant. Tell me what the doctor said," Jeremiah told her, abruptly changing the conversation.

"But *Daed,* I will be fine soon. You did not need to hire anyone, especially not an outsider!" Kayla cried.

Jeremiah's mouth became a fine line and his eyes narrowed.

"I do not wish to discuss the Englisher," he told her flatly. "I asked you about the doctor. What was said and what tests were done?"

Kayla swallowed another question.

"She believes that it is a blood disorder of sorts but I will not know until the tests come back. Simple bloodwork was performed. I will return next week for the results."

Jeremiah's brow knitted and he nodded.

"What sort of blood disorder?"

Kayla shrugged.

"I do not know, Daed. She did not give me specifics. I can only wait to learn."

Jeremiah did not seem happy with her answer but Kayla had little else to give him.

"Go rest now, Kayla. I will come to you after the work is done."

"*Daed*, may I go for Hannah? I do not wish to spend one more minute in bed. Please?"

Jeremiah regarded her for a long moment before bobbing his head reluctantly.

"If you are certain you are not feeling ill, you may pick up your sister from school. But you must come straight back to bed. Understood?"

Gratefully, Kayla nodded and hurried toward the front door before he could change his mind.

It will be lovely to stretch my legs and inhale the fresh autumn air, she thought. She was beginning to feel as a caged rabbit.

As she walked toward the road, she found herself looking back at Will Jenkins. He was hard at work, paying her no mind but as she turned in the direction of the schoolhouse, Kayla thought she could feel eyes on her.

Who is this man and what is he doing here?

That evening, Lydia Fisher came as promised, preparing a delicious supper for the Roths before heading home to her own family.

"She is a blessing to us," Jeremiah commented when she left and they sat down to eat. Kayla scowled slightly.

"She really doesn't need be here quite so often, *Daed*," she told her father. "I can still work."

"Your health is paramount, Kayla. Lydia has four able sons to work their farm and can spare a hand until you are well."

"I am well!" Kayla grunted, trying to keep the frustration from her voice. Jeremiah shot her a warning look and Kayla clamped her mouth closed. Arguing would not prove fruitful.

"Tell me about the Englisher," Kayla said instead and Hannah's head jerked upward from her stew.

"What Englisher?" the little girl asked curiously. Jeremiah's scowl deepened and he shook his head almost imperceivably at his oldest daughter.

"I have already explained that Will is helping with the harvest. There is nothing else to tell."

"Where did you find him, *Daed*? You must admit that it is odd to bring an outsider here when there are many in the community whom you could call upon for help."

Jeremiah's blue eyes seemed to darken.

"I am the head of this house," he snapped. "I do not need to answer to you for my choices."

Kayla was stung by his tone and she bit her lower lip. It was unlike her father to speak crossly to her or Hannah.

Whatever silliness is happening with me is causing him stress, she determined, taking a spoonful of beef stew. *I must not give him more of a reason to worry.*

She did not mention Will again but she decided that she would speak to Will the next time she saw him and learn more about him.

Kayla had her chance the following day. Jeremiah went to sell their goods at market, leaving Kayla alone.

"I have asked Lydia to come later in the day to ensure you are well," her father told her. Kayla rolled her eyes where he could not see.

You must not get annoyed, she warned herself but she could not help but feel frustrated at being treated like a child. She knew that was not Jeremiah's intention but she could not release the slight resentment she was feeling.

Her mother had died when she was fourteen, leaving Kayla as the woman of the household. Hannah was still an infant and Kayla had learned to tend to both the baby and the farm.

Standing idle was not something which she did well and she wished desperately that the doctors would quickly diagnose her issue so she was able to resume her role in the family and on the farm.

"Thank you, *Daed,*" she said instead of unleashing the barrage of protests vying to spring from her lips.

"I do not want you to leave the house today, Kayla," Jeremiah told her seriously as he stood in the doorway of her bedroom. "Stay inside and preferably in bed. If you are to faint with no one nearby..."

"I will not faint!" she cried but Jeremiah shook his head.

"You have no way of assuring me of that," he replied. "Please heed my words, Kayla. I speak only out of concern for you."

Begrudgingly, Kayla nodded.

"Yes, *Daed,*" she agreed. "I will take Hannah to school and – "

"No," Jeremiah said sharply. "Lydia will take your sister to school."

Kayla gritted her teeth and nodded.

"Have a good day in town, *Daed,*" Kayla sighed. She watched as he retreated to the freshly loaded wagon and disappeared down the road.

I have become a prisoner in my own home, Kayla thought mournfully, folding her arms across her chest. She wondered what she would do for the remainder of the day and as she thought it, she watched a silver sedan car driving up the road which Jeremiah had just taken.

Kayla leaned forward, watching the dilapidated vehicle pull onto their land, her pulse quickening. As she peered at the driver, she realized it was Will Jenkins arriving to work.

Is he supposed to be here today? She wondered nervously. If so, why hadn't her father told her to expect him.

Will jumped from the driver's seat and she noted he was wearing the same clothes he had the day before. He did not seem to notice her observing him, pulling a few items which she could not see from the backseat before turning toward the barn.

As Kayla rose her hand to wave in greeting, something tugged on her skirt.

"Kayla, I am hungry!" Hannah announced from behind her, causing the older girl to jump.

"You startled me, Hannah!" she chided and Hannah shrugged indifferently. She turned to usher her sister into the house, eyeing Will who had vanished behind the house.

I wonder if I should tend to him, she thought but her father's words reverberated in her mind.

"I do not want you to leave the house today, Kayla. Stay inside and preferably in bed. If you are to faint with no one nearby..."

She pushed the thought of Will Jenkins from her mind and closed the door.

She had no reason to approach the Englisher.

The weather had turned unseasonably warm and Kayla lifted her head from her book, realizing that the front room had grown almost stifling hot.

She cast the novel aside and reached to open the window, gazing into the fields. To her surprise, she saw Will Jenkins standing near the maple tree beside his car, wiping sweat from his brow.

Kayla watched him for a moment and she could see the sun and hard work had turned his face red.

He must be thirsty. He is dressed much too warmly to work the fields in that attire, she realized, rising from window seat.

A cool glass of water in hand, Kayla stepped into the yard. Will's back was to her and she tried to make herself heard as to not surprise him.

He turned and Kayla was filled with a strange sense of familiarity suddenly, something she had not felt the previous afternoon.

"Hello," he said and Kayla nodded, handing him the glass of water.

"It is very hot today," she volunteered. "I thought you might be thirsty."

He nodded gratefully and accepted the beverage, drinking it in one long gulp.

"I will fetch you another one," she offered and he shook his head.

"No, thank you," he replied. "I should be getting back to work."

He was older than Kayla with dark hair and vivid green eyes. His face seemed it had not been shaved in four days and there were dark circles under his eyes.

He is handsome in a rugged sort of way, she thought, studying his face. The feeling that she knew him did not diminish.

"As you wish," she replied, turning back.

"Actually wait," Will called nervously. He peered at his gloved hands in embarrassment as Kayla turned back to him.

"Yes?"

"Maybe one more glass of water," he muttered and Kayla smiled.

"Of course."

Inside the house, she thought of the somewhat bedraggled man on her lawn and she again wondered where he had come from.

If he has no water, he likely has no food either, she realized and quickly went to work preparing him a snack. *If he doesn't eat, he will also faint. Daed doesn't need to come home to such a sight.*

She did not want to think what her father would say if he knew she was feeding the Englisher.

Outside, she gestured for him to sit and eat. The gratitude in his face was beyond anything she had ever seen and a mixture of sadness and pity overwhelmed her.

"Are you from Lancaster, Mr. Jenkins?" Kayla asked timidly as he inhaled the bread and cheese she had brought to him. He shook his head and she waited for him to swallow the morsels before answering.

"No," he replied. "I am from Reading."

Kayla's brow furrowed.

"Reading?" she asked in surprise. "You have a little bit of a journey to make here."

Will nodded and shrugged his shoulders.

"It is an hour's drive," he answered. "But your father offered me very good pay and gas money for the trip."

None of what he said made sense to Kayla.

Why would Daed bring an Englisher to the district from an hour away?

"You know, I don't even know your name," Will commented as he polished off the last of the light meal she provided for him.

Embarrassed, Kayla extended her hand.

"Kayla Roth."

Will accepted her outstretched palm and they two looked at one another for a long moment. Kayla felt a sudden confusion as she stared at him.

Why do I feel such an affinity with this man? She wondered, an almost awe-struck feeling overcoming her.

"Nice to meet you, Kayla. I should be getting back to work. I don't want your dad to think he's wasting his money."

Kayla stepped back reluctantly, wanting to speak with him longer but she knew he was right. There was much work to be done and she had detained the harvest enough already.

"If you should need more water, Mr. Jenkins," Kayla told him. "There is a spigot beside the barn."

He looked at her thankfully.

"You truly are a lifesaver, Miss Roth. You and your father have helped me a great deal already."

Kayla did not know how to respond but Will did not seem to require an answer.

She slipped back into the house and reclaimed her window seat but her book was forgotten. She spent the remainder of the afternoon watching Will working in the field and wondering if *Gotte* had sent him to their farm for a reason.

Kayla waited impatiently for her father to take Hannah to school before hurrying outside to greet Will who was cleaning the stalls. Her father would not be gone long but she wanted to talk to the man again, if only for a short time.

"Good morning, Miss Roth," Will said brightly. She smiled.

"You may call me Kayla," she told him. "I brought you muffins if you are hungry."

She offered them to him and he took them happily. For the third day, he donned the same clothes and Kayla wondered if he had any other garments.

He is obviously not well off. I wonder if that is why Daed brought him here; to help a man down on his luck.

"In that case, you can call me Will," he laughed, taking a bite of the muffin in his hand. His dark eyebrows shot up.

"This is great!" he said. "Did you make this yourself?"

She nodded.

"The Amish can do everything," he sighed. "I knew an Amish girl once. She never failed to amaze me with her talents."

"What happened to her?" Kayla asked curiously, leaning against a stall door. Will smiled thinly.

"She returned to her community. Decided the outside world wasn't for her after all."

Kayla could read the regret in his face but before she could ask anything else, she felt herself grow lightheaded.

Oh no! She thought as bright lights colored her line of sight.

"Kayla?" Will's voice sounded very far away and suddenly she was in his arms as her legs buckled beneath her. She willed herself to take deep breaths and to her relief she did not faint.

"Are you all right?" Will demanded as she regained her footing. Slowly he released her and Kayla stood on shaking legs.

She nodded, shifting her eyes downward.

"I get fainting spells sometimes," she confessed as the spots cleared from her vision. Will's emerald eyes narrowed.

"Have you been to the doctor?" he asked and Kayla bobbed her head.

"I am awaiting test results," she told him, sighing. "They believe it is some sort of blood disorder."

Will's mouth became a tight, white line.

"Is that so?" he asked quietly.

"Kayla! What are you doing in here?" Jeremiah appeared in the doorway, his face pale as he took in the scene before him.

"I – I came to offer Mr. Jenkins some muffins," she murmured, averting her eyes from his shocked face.

"You should not be in here," he told his daughter, shooing her from the barn.

"Thank you for the muffins, Kayla," Will called after her. "I hope you are feeling better."

Jeremiah led the way back to the house and did not say a word until they were inside, whirling to confront Kayla.

"Why were you speaking with Will Jenkins?" he demanded furiously. "I told you that you are to stay in the house."

"Daed, I am growing mad staying in the house!" Kayla protested. "And Will seems a very nice man!"

Jeremiah's expression was indecipherable as he stared at his oldest daughter. He seemed to be considering his next words carefully.

"You are to stay away from Will Jenkins," he told her firmly. "I do not want you anywhere near him, do you understand?"

Kayla's eyebrows knit together.

"No," she answered truthfully. "Of course I do not understand. Why would you ask me to stay away from him?"

"He is not someone whom you should associate yourself," Jeremiah insisted. Kayla stared at him uncomprehendingly.

"*Daed*, if he is such a terrible man, why would you have him come to our home?"

"He not in our home. He is merely helping with harvest. I want you to swear that you will not have any further contact with him. Swear it, Kayla!"

Kayla did not know what to say. She wanted to promise her father that she wouldn't see the Englisher again but she knew her curiosity would not keep her away.

"Kayla!"

She hung her head and nodded, sighing deeply.

"I swear it, *Daed*," she breathed but she wondered if she would be able to honor her oath.

Kayla did not risk going to Will until the next time her father went to the market, three days later. She found herself watching the worker from the window often, willing him to take notice of her and sometimes he would lift his head and acknowledge her with a half-wave but never in Jeremiah's presence.

This makes little sense. Daed brings him from out of town to work and then speaks as if the man is a danger to us.

The previous day, she had gone to the hospital for her test results.

"As we suspected, Kayla, you have a blood disorder called megaloblastic anemia. It can be treated with supplements and dietary changes but it is manageable," the doctor informed her. Kayla nodded, relieved the diagnosis was simple.

"When will I be able to resume my work?" she asked eagerly and the doctor chuckled.

"We will start your injections immediately and you should notice a change within a week or so. The fatigue and dizziness will lessen and you will be back to normal in no time."

Kayla peered at the physician.

"What causes this?" she asked with interest.

"In your case, it is genetic," the doctor replied.

After Hannah left for school and her father for the market, Kayla rushed outside to speak with Will.

"Kayla, you should not be out here," he told her, his jaw locking when she appeared. Kayla was hurt by his words.

"I do not understand; why does my father wish to keep me away from you?" she asked bluntly but Will did not answer as he continued to bale hay.

"I'm sorry," she muttered, turning away. "I only came to tell you that I got my results from the hospital. I have a blood disorder – anemia."

Will's head jerked up to stare at her, his mouth open slightly.

"What kind of anemia?" he demanded. Kayla wracked her mind to recall the proper term.

"Mega...mega..."

"Megaloblastic?"

Kayla smiled.

"Yes, that is it."

Kayla waited for him to return her grin but his face went dark.

"You should go back in the house. You don't want your father to catch you out here."

She stared at him, tears of humiliation filling her eyes.

I thought we had a bond, she thought miserably, chewing on her lower lip.

"Hurry up," Will growled, pointing at the house. Kayla spun, tears spilling down her cheeks as she ran back inside.

Daed was right; I should have just stayed away from him.

"Kayla! *Daed* is yelling!" Hannah cried, flying into the kitchen where Kayla was doing the dishes.

"What?"

"He is yelling at the Englisher!" Hannah insisted, pointing toward the front of the house. Kayla quickly dried her hands on her apron and rushed toward the door. As she pulled open the heavy wood, she heard a car door slam and watched as Will screeched away in his rundown sedan.

Jeremiah stood, his arms folded angrily across his chest as he watched the man leave and Kayla was sure she had never seen him look so intimidating.

"*Daed*! *Daed,* what happened?" she cried, rushing toward him. He whirled to face her, his face undergoing several expressions, settling on near-panic.

"Nothing," he replied gruffly. "Go inside."

"*Daed* please!" she begged. "What happened with Will?"

His eyes narrowed dangerously and he shook his head.

"I made a mistake bringing him here," he muttered, storming toward the house. "Do not mention his name in this house again."

Bewildered, Kayla turned toward the road but of course Will was long gone.

She looked helplessly at her father but she was only staring at his retreating back and Kayla was filled with an inexplicable sense of loss.

He is not coming back, she realized and the thought made her sick to her stomach for reasons she could not comprehend.

Life on the Roth farm returned to normal and as promised, Kayla began to feel better as the treatments took effect.

The harvest went well and Will Jenkins did not return to the district but his memory was fresh in Kayla's mind.

Perhaps one day, Daed will tell me who he was truly and how he came to be here. But she did not have high hopes for that occurring. Jeremiah never brought up the Englisher again and Kayla did not dare.

It was the beginning of November when the letter arrived.

It was slipped between the screen door and it had not been mailed.

Without opening it, Kayla suspected she knew who had written it but as she tore into the envelope, her suspicions were confirmed.

Her hands trembling, she read the letter, her heart thumping wildly.

Dear Kayla, it read. *I have wrestled with whether to write this letter or leave well enough alone as your father wanted. I can't live my life without telling you who I am because I think you deserve the truth. As you know, my name is William Jenkins. Twenty years ago, I met a beautiful girl in Lancaster and we fell madly in love. I mentioned that I once knew an Amish girl and that girl was your mother, Anna. We had plans to marry but one day, I woke up and she was gone. She had left me a letter, much like the one I am writing you, apologizing for her choice and claiming she had made a mistake leaving her community. She begged me not to look for her and I agreed. I left town and moved to Reading, not wanting to run into her. If I had stayed, I would have learned that she married Jeremiah Roth and soon gave birth to a beautiful baby daughter; you.*

If I had not seen your eyes, I may never have known that you were mine but there is no mistaking you are my child.

I did not understand why your father had brought me to your farm until I heard you were sick. Megaloblastic anemia is genetic – I know because I have it also. I suspect Jeremiah was terribly concerned for your health and wanted to learn about your family history. I don't think he ever intended for us to meet and when we did and I learned the truth, he grew angry and banished me from the farm. I want you to know that if I had known you were my child, I would have always been in your life.

You may do what you wish with this information, Kayla. You may choose to never see me again or you may confront your father. Shamefully I do not know you well enough to know how you will react but I would like to get to know you. You are a grown woman and I can't force a relationship on you.

Whatever you do, please remember that your father only did what he did to keep you safe, happy and healthy. If you decide to let him know that you know, go easy on him. He is the only father you have ever had after all.

I have enclosed my phone number and mailing address. I will not hold my breath but I will hold onto hope that you will see me again.

Whatever you choose, know that I support you and love you. I wish you only the best this world has to offer.

Love always,

Will

Tears flowed freely down Kayla's face and the words grew blurry as she read and re-read the letter, her breath escaping in shuddering sobs.

"Oh Gotte, Kayla!" Jeremiah cried, entering the foyer where his oldest daughter stood. "What happened?"

Kayla shook her head and stuffed the letter back into the envelope, wiping her face with the back of her hand.

"Nothing, nothing," she gasped. He stared at her, his face a mask of worry and Kayla had never been filled with so much love for another person.

Does he know I know? Has he been filled with worry for the past nineteen years that the truth would come out and he would lose the daughter he had raised as his own? Kayla could not imagine the pain her father must have endured over the years.

He is the only father I have ever known. He is my Daed no matter what that letter reads.

Impulsively, she threw herself into her father's arm, burying her face in his broad chest.

"I love you, *Daed*," she whispered, inhaling the comforting scent of his dirty work clothes.

"I love you, daughter," he sighed.

In that moment, Kayla knew she would honor her father's wishes and never again bring up Will Jenkin's name in their home.

That did not mean she would never see the Englisher again.

END

SMALL TOWN CHURCH ROMANCE

66

CHELSEA BECKS

"YOU WILL GO TO HELL. THE POWER OF CHRIST COMPELS YOU. THE POWER OF CHRIST WILL SAVE YOU IF YOU BELIEVE IN HIM. THE POWER OF CHRIST WILL KEEP YOU FROM HELL. GET YOUR ACT TOGETHER AND BELIEVE IN GOD."

Sara was a little freaked out.

Okay . . . Sara was really freaked out.

"So my cousin is a pharmacist and she can totally sneak me some Valium for this guy," Miranda, next to her, whispered in her ear.

Sara only went to church because it was routine. That wasn't to say she wasn't a pretty good Christian; she never killed anybody and she didn't eat meat on Fridays. Sometimes she prayed before she went to bed, and she never said the Lord's name in vain. Well. She tried not to.

"Look at that vein that bulges in his neck," Sara whispered to Miranda.

"Watch it burst," Miranda said smugly.

Sara tried not to smile.

No one in the congregation was okay with Pastor Henry being a total freak show. In fact it was completely surprising that their old pastor, Pastor Samuel, had picked him for his replacement at all. The young guy was new in town, and seemed to be totally normal, but how did he pass the job interview? Sara imagined Pastor Samuel in Boca or wherever he was, having a good laugh about his little practical joke, before informing all of them that the real Pastor would start next Sunday.

"He's kind of cute," Callie, from the other side of Miranda, said.

"Gross," Sara and Miranda said in unison.

Pastor Henry didn't hear any of this. "DO YOU THINK WHAT YOU ARE DOING IS OKAY? DO YOU REALIZE JESUS DIED FOR ALL OF YOU AND ALL YOU DO IS DISOBEY THE WORD OF GOD. REAL CLASSY. REALLY REALLY CLASSY. JUST YOU WAIT. JUST YOU WAIT FOR THE GLORIOUS DAYS OF REVELATION! YOU KNOW THE RIVER? THE TOWN RIVER? I WANT YOU ALL THERE TOMORROW AT SUNSET! THERE I WILL REPENT YOU OF YOUR SINS AND YOU WON'T ROT IN HELL LIKE YOU SHOULD!"

"Pop," Miranda whispered.

"TO QUOTE REVELATION:
BUT THE FEARFUL, AND UNBELIEVING, AND THE ABOMINABLE, AND MURDERERS, AND WHORE MONGERS, AND SORCERERS, AND IDOLATERS, AND ALL LIARS, SHALL HAVE THEIR PART IN THE LAKE WHICH BURNETH WITH FIRE AND BRIMSTONE: WHICH IS THE SECOND DEATH!

AVOID THE SECOND DEATH MY PARISHIONERS. AVOID THE SECOND DEATH AND FIND JESUS IN YOUR HEART. MEET ME AT

THE RIVER AT SUNSET. THE RIVER AT SUNSET. BE THERE OR ROT IN HELL!"

After church, everyone usually met in the hall for coffee hour. The girls did as not to say no to free food, but they noticed the crowd was a little thinner than usual.

"I wonder if he's gonna keep screaming?" Miranda asked, helping herself to a donut.

"It was kind of hot," Callie said.

"You're weird. You two deserve each other in hell."

The girls were then interrupted by the presence of Miss Hattie: the church clerk who was as wide as she was tall . . . and she was pretty tall. She plowed right between the group and helped herself to two donuts. "Hey, girls!" she said, the natural volume of her voice set to "loud". Her church dress that she wore every week was a dusty rose color with bright blue flowers and purple polka dots, her gray hair set in curls around her face.

"Hey, Miss Hattie," the three said in unison.

"Isn't it nice that even though your parents are dead all you girls still come to church?" She smiled brightly.

"Our parents aren't dead," Callie said, acknowledging herself and Sara.

"And my parents have been dead my whole life." Miranda had lived with her aunt and uncle since she was a baby.

"Oh." It was clear that Miss Hattie's memory was evading her, but she would never admit it. She smiled, and the girls noticed a streak of lipstick on her front teeth. "Well, anyway, we like to see young folk in the congregation."

"Is that why Pastor Samuel appointed a young minister?" Sara wondered. If anyone was going to spill the details on the parish's opinion of Pastor Henry it was going to be Miss Hattie.

Miss Hattie pursed her lips. "Well, now, you see I told Pastor Samuel that appointing a woman wouldn't be a bad idea. You know Rose Becker? Her daughter Lucy has just gotten her license or whatever they call it and she's a wonderful preacher, has a presence, and she's not too pretty so following the word of God might be able to find her someone. Anyway, I suggested to Pastor Samuel to appoint Lucy, and did he listen to me? Nope! He just appointed Henry, and I gotta say girls, he's a bit too aggressive for my liking."

The girls nodded in agreement, and Sara was grateful Callie didn't mention how cute she thought he was.

Before the conversation could progress, Pastor Henry was next to them. Close up, Sara noticed he wasn't a bad looking guy. He had dusty blonde hair, brown eyes, and nice features. He didn't look the least bit scary at all up close. He didn't even having the vein popping out of his neck.

"Hello," he said. Even his voice was quiet. "I'm just trying to go around and meet everyone."

"Well, you already met me," Miss Hattie said, clearly offended.

"Yes, Miss Hattie, I have met you." He even smiled, and Sara noticed it was a nice smile. "And you are all . . ?

"Calliope Calavant," Callie said. She completely made that up. Her real name was Callie Smith, but whenever she was meeting a new guy she liked to sound exotic.

"Miranda," Miranda said. "I don't have a last name."

Sara decided that since they were in a church she should be honest. "Sara Clevenger," she said. "Nice to meet you."

"Nice to meet all of you." Henry nodded. "I hope to see you all at the river tomorrow night. It really will be a fun time."

"Can you promise that?" Callie asked. The other two rolled their eyes.

"Yes," he laughed, but Sara noticed that Henry was looking at her when he said it. "I can promise that."

The girls went to brunch like they usually did on Sundays, and then Sara rushed home. Her mother had just left for work, picking up an extra shift at the bar she worked at, which meant her father was alone. He couldn't be that way for too long.

"Hey dad," Sarah said. Her father, Bill, was sitting in the recliner watching TV, his wheelchair next to him. He was dressed in his usual sweatpants and black T-shirt, his mouth open slightly as he looked at his daughter. He smiled. "Did you eat lunch yet?"

Bill managed a little nod. He couldn't speak. He had ALS, a diagnoses that tore Sara's family apart emotionally, but they still managed to stay together. Sara moved back home while her mother worked more to help take care of her dad.

"Are you comfy?" Sara asked, but then proceeded to fluff the pillow behind his back a little more. She looked at the TV. He was watching the baseball game, so at least he was actually entertained and not faking it for the amusement of his wife.

"Are you OK?" Sara asked.

Bill looked at her, and nodded. Sara couldn't help but smile at her father. "Okay," she said.

Henry lived in the rectory next to the church. He never had to pay rent and it was well lined so it was never too cold. He liked making a fire and drank tea every night while doing his Bible readings.

As he read that night, his mind flicked back to church. He knew his methods were extreme, but his favorite pastor had the same approach and where he grew up everyone loved the way that he preached. He wasn't sure how the new church felt about it, however. They all looked a little scared.

He then thought about Sara. The other two girls she was with were pretty, but there was something about her that really stood out to him. Maybe because she didn't have that pinched look on her face like Miranda, or because she didn't immediately try to jump in his pants like Callie. She was calm, and polite, and . . . beautiful.

He wasn't too sure about the meeting at the river the next day, but he was positive that she would show up. She did look interested when he mentioned it . . . unless he totally imagined that she did.

Henry looked out the window, wrapping his fingers around his warm tea cup and watched as the sun began to set. His street had the most perfect view of the horizon. He wondered if Sara liked sunsets.

Henry shook his head, and hoped that she would show up to the river. He hoped that she would like it. He hoped the whole town would.

That night, after Sara had put Bill to bed, her mother Nancy came home, finding Sara in the kitchen doing dishes. Nancy was a woman that aged too quickly. Having a dying spouse would do that to you. She was still pretty though, with blonde hair like her only daughter, and blue eyes. She worked hard at the bar, and made pretty good money. She needed to to take care of Bill.

"Hungry?" Sara asked. "I made Dad scrambled eggs. I could whip you up some."

Nancy collapsed at the table and shook her head. "I ate at work. How did he do?"

Sara bit her lip. "He didn't eat much. He tried to, but I don't think he was that hungry."

Nancy nodded, not bothering to hide how unbelievable exhausted she was. "How was church? The new preacher started today, didn't he?

"He wants to dunk us all in the river to repent us of our sins," Sara said, dropping the plate she was holding as the water suddenly got really hot. She turned down the dial and braved to pick it up again. "He's pretty crazy. He screamed the entire time instead of just giving a normal sermon. It was really uncomfortable."

"He probably just doesn't understand the way we are used to things." Nancy always tried to sympathize with things that were generally not well liked. Her favorite animal was the opossum.

"Or he's crazy," Sara laughed.

"I want you to go to that river dunk thing tomorrow," Nancy said. "Just give it a try. It's important we support members of the community. That church has helped us out so much since your father got sick, it's the least you could do."

Sara didn't want to argue with her mother. She didn't want to go, but she knew that if it was important to Nancy than it should be important to her. She decided not to ask Miranda and Callie if they were going too. She didn't want to get laughed at.

At seven o'clock the next evening, Henry waited by the river. It was the main water source in town, leading right into the reservoir. He figured the river would be a good place for the re-baptism of the congregation. He loved water. He loved its healing spirit. He hoped everyone else would too .No one was there yet, but he realized that "sunset" was a bit of a vague time. Maybe everyone else did not read the same solar clock he did and would be there in a little bit. He checked his watch. 7:01.

At quarter after, he checked his watch for the umpteenth time. No one was there yet. Henry could feel his smile begin to fade.

7:30, the sun was beginning to be a peachy color, and night was beginning to overtake the sky when he heard the car pull up. It parked on the grass, and the driver got out. It took him a second to realize it was Sara, and suddenly it did not matter that no one else in the congregation had showed up to the baptism.

"Pastor Henry," she said.

"It's just Henry."

She nodded. "Henry."

"Sara."

"Are you going to scream at me while you dunk me in the river, or is it completely okay if I just go about and do this myself?"

He felt a little uneasy. "I can give you a blessing," he said. "And I promise I won't scream."

She took off her shirt, and while the motion caught him off guard, Henry realized that she was wearing a one piece bathing suit. She stripped off her jean, and stood on the grass, curling it under her toes. He then took off his pants to his swim suit, and hesitated about his shirt, before realizing that it really didn't matter, then took it off. He was happy that for the first time in his life he was actually in somewhat good of shape, then realized how wrong it was of him to be thinking like that when he was about to baptize someone.

Him and Sara walked toward the river. He dunked his foot in, and realized the water was just a little bit warmer than ice. This would be quick. Sara, meanwhile, did not hesitate. She plunged right in, under the water, the light current not swaying her a bit. She resurfaced, and slicked her wet hair off her face with her hands before smiling. "Was that too premature for a blessing?" she asked.

"No," Henry replied, awing at how beautiful she looked in the sunset.

"It's better just to go right in," she explained. "Otherwise you'll be shivering. This way your body gets used to it."

Henry supposed she was right. He hadn't swam since summer camp when he was a kid; and even then he barely ever did. He was too busy reading a book to socialize with the other kids. Henry had never been much of a people person, even as a child. He turned to the church and his faith and the pastor who taught him so much, and only then was he able to find any comfort in himself.

Henry decided to just go for it, and dove right into the icy water, feeling it seep through his skin and freeze his veins. When he came up for air, he gasped, and then registered that Sara was laughing at him. He stood up, and shook his hair, before saying, "How the hell did you do that?"

"Did you just say hell?" she mused.

"I'm human, you know," he muttered.

Sara grinned. "Okay, so this baptism or whatever . . . let's just do this."

Henry nodded, then waded through the water so that he was standing right next to Sara. "I do this for you. I do this for your soul."

She nodded, and maybe he was imagining it, but she seemed to be staring at him.

"I'm going to dip your head in the water now."

She was treading in the shallow water, and he held her forehead as she dipped her hair under the water. He tried not to run his fingers through her hair. He tried to be professional, as he recited:

Living and Loving Father,
I praise and thank You with my heart for the liberation You
have given me from the clutches of sin and Satan. By Your
death on the Cross of Calvary, You have put my old life with its
sin and judgment to death forever, and endowed me with a
new life that is abounding with joy.
Father, I commit this Baptism Day into Your most precious
and loving hands. I believe that by Your crucifixion on the
Cross, my old self was rendered powerless and I was freed from
all sin. You were raised from the dead that I too may live a life
victorious and overcoming all evil.
Father, this day, I rededicate myself to live in You and live a
life for Your glory. I remember the day when I was baptized
and washed off all my sins. Lord, it is Your grace that I must be
counted worthy to be called Your child. Help me to keep Your
commandments. Renew my strength this day that I may be
strong in faith and increase in zeal. Preserve me for the
glorious day of Your coming. I believe Your Word which says,
"He who has begun a good work in you will complete it until
the day of Jesus Christ." Let this day be the beginning. Lead me
into greater spiritual depths even in the coming days. In Jesus'
precious name I pray.
Amen.

Henry traced the cross on her forehead with his thumb. "Amen," he whispered again, and then gently helped Sara lift her head up.

They locked eyes for a second, and that was when Henry noticed his hand was around her waist. Sara noticed too, but she did not try to stop it, in fact she felt like it should be there.

"So I'm not going to hell?" she whispered.

"No way," he whispered back.

Before he could acknowledge that it was happening, he was kissing her, or was she kissing him? They were kissing each other, and behind them the sun officially set.

The darkness over came the river, and noticing that their visibility was waning, Sara and Henry stopped before getting out of the river. Henry did not know what to say to her, other than a slew of apologies that was normal for him to spurt out in this type of situation. However, instead, he noticed she was smiling and said, "Was that okay?"

Sara laughed. "That was fine."

She realized she didn't bring a towel, so she put her clothes on over her soaking wet bathing suit. Henry put on his shirt, and then felt a little awkward about the situation. Even though kissing Sara was better than he imagined, he realized then he really did not know her at all, and to her he was just the screaming preacher.

"I'm sorry." His familiar words came out of his mouth.

"I kissed you," she said, giving him a weird look.

"I thought I kissed you?"

They were quiet for a second, and then both laughed.

Sara didn't expect any of that to happen, except for maybe the fact that she would be the only one to show up for the baptism ritual by the river. Flushed, and feeling happy for whatever reason, she went home to shower, and then proceeded to get ready for a night out with Callie and Miranda.

They all met at their favorite restaurant outside of town, where on Mondays the cocktails were half price after nine. Miranda wore a low cut sweater, and Callie an even tighter one. Sara tried not to smile to broadly when she sat down at the table.

"Who did you lay?" Callie asked.

"No one," Sara muttered, taking a sip of the martini her friends had already ordered her. She knew how the others felt about Henry, and since she didn't know if she really liked him yet she figured she should maybe keep the events of the evening to herself.

"Boring." Miranda rolled her eyes.

They all ordered a variety of appetizers, and the conversation as usual took a turn to talking about hot men. A little tipsy, Sara tried her best to keep her mouth shut, but eventually she was dying with curiosity.

"Henry is pretty hot," she said.

"Pastor Henry?" Callie asked. "Hell yeah."

"Nope." Miranda winced and shook her head. "Absolutely not. Nuh uh. No way."

"I think I like him," Sara said, and then she slurped her martini instead of looking at her friends for their reactions. When she deemed enough time had passed, she dared a glance, and saw both of them with their mouths wide open, not unlike a fish above water.

"Don't do it!" Miranda warned.

"Don't!"

"Think of your father!"

"Think of the women and children!"

"He's CRAZY!"

"ABSOLUTELY insane!"

"Even Miss Hattie didn't like him!"

It was clear that Miranda and Callie were getting hysterical. Around them, other people in the restaurant began to stare, and Sara was getting more and more uncomfortable. She was not expecting this much of an outburst.

"Okay, okay!" Sara held her hand up to silence them. "Keep your pants on. I won't do anything about it."

Although her friends looked relieved, deep inside Sara felt a little hurt. She tried not to imagine kissing Henry for the rest of the reason, but she found it really hard not to.

Henry was sitting in his office the next day writing a sermon when he heard the knock on the door. "Come in," he said.

The door opened, and he didn't bother to look up, figuring it was just Miss Hattie, when a familiar and beautiful voice said, "We need to talk."

He looked up and saw Sara there. She was wearing a dress, her hair tied back, and even though she wasn't dripping wet in the sunset she was still beautiful. Henry thought she may be too good to be true. "Sara," he said. "Come in."

She did, which he took as a good sign. He was glad he cleaned off his desk that morning; he didn't want her thinking he was a slob. Sara sighed. "We have to talk . . . about your preaching."

"You don't like it?" he asked.

"You're a little . . . aggressive," Sara said, and then she bit her lip. "It's scaring all of your friends."

"You're scared of what your friends think?" Maybe Sara was one of those shallow girls that Henry had known growing up. He couldn't help but feel a pit of disappointment form in his stomach.

"My friends . . . the town . . ." Sara winced. "You're just so different from Pastor Samuel. He was gentle and sweet and at first I thought that maybe the aggressive and angry, brimstone and fire speech was just what you were, but after what happened at the river . . . you're a nice guy, Henry. You're kind and charming and the person who baptized me and the person who was screaming Revelation were not the same person."

"Pastor Samuel knew what he was hiring," Henry said, feeling a little angry. "He knew what my style was and he liked it and when I was hired . . . he knew what he was getting."

"We don't know if it was a joke though."

Sara regretted it the moment she said it. Henry, meanwhile, did not know her well enough to figure that out. He stood up and pointed to the door. "I think you should leave."

"Henry . . ."

"Now."

She stood up and made her way to the door. Before she left though, she turned around and said, "I really liked the kissing, by the way. I really like you."

And with that, she left, and Henry was more confused and hurt than ever.

Sara cried in the car on the way home, to get it out of her system before she saw her father and she had to be strong for him. She wiped her face, and reapplied her mascara, before going inside the house. Her father was sleeping in his wheelchair in the kitchen; the warmest room in the house because of the sunlight that swallowed the room through the big bay window.

She decided not to disturb him, and made herself a peanut butter and jelly sandwich. As she ate, she watched her father. His chest was rising and falling slowly; he was still breathing. She knew she only had months more with him, and dreaded the moment when his chest would no longer rise and fall and he would be nothing more than a memory. His disease was always fatal, and there was nothing she could do about it but enjoy the time she had left with him.

When she was done eating, Bill opened his eyes.

"Hey, Dad," she said.

He tried to smile.

"I think I might have done something stupid.

When her father was functional, the two were close. Now, however, since he could not spill all of her secrets to the world, Sara found herself telling him everything that was on her mind. Since he could smile and sometimes shake his head, it was a sort of effective way of communication. It made her feel better at least.

"I kissed the pastor."

Bill opened his eyes wider.

"Not Pastor Samuel. Pastor Henry. The new pastor. He's young, and kind, and super socially awkward . . . he's a really great guy. I can tell. But he's a yeller. He screams about Satan and he wanted to dunk everyone in the river to repent their sins and . . . no one likes him. No one. Not Miranda or Callie or Miss Hattie . . ."

Bill didn't say anything, or even react.

"I don't know what to do, Dad."

Suddenly, Sara thought her father was choking. He started making noise, and she ran over to him, but Bill tried to push her aside as best as he could. She stopped, and looked at her father, and his eyes widened a little more. "Give," he stammered. "Him. A Ch-ch-chance."

Sara teared up: her father hadn't spoken in over a month. "Dad?"

He coughed a little, and then swallowed, and nodded., then smiled.

"Give him a chance?"

Bill nodded.

If it had been any other person besides her father, who had used all of her strength to tell her that, she most likely would have ignored it. "Okay," Sara nodded, still teared up. "I will."

Henry thought a lot about what Sara had told him, and as much as he did not want to listen to a woman and do what she told him to do, he also had to take in account what was best for his congregation.

He arranged a meeting with Miss Hattie and, just like Sara had told him, she agreed that his sermons needed to die down a little bit. Henry called up Pastor Samuel, who said that hiring Henry was not a joke, but he hoped that he would learn his lesson and arrange his sermons to be friendlier. He also wished Henry luck with Sara, and hoped the best for him.

Henry spent the last few days of the week to write Sunday's sermon. He hoped Sara and the rest of the congregation would like it.

On Sunday, he dressed in his robes, and began the service. He spoke quietly, but not too quiet, and tried not to let his nerves get the best of him. He tried not to look at Sara too much, but there she was: sitting in the second row with her wretched friends, a small smile on her face the entire time.

Then, it was time for the sermon. Again, he spoke quietly, and firmly, and then when it was close to an end, he said, "I am new in town. I am a new preacher, and you are a new community. As many of you know Jesus was a stranger in many lands amongst his travels, and although his methods weren't as . . . extreme . . . as mine, he did get some ridicule. But there were also those that gave him a chance, and those who helped him become well known and lead him down the road for him to help him save us. I want us all to grow as a community and to become followers of Jesus and God together, so today, I propose that after service we all go down to the river and pray together, and wash away all of our sins and start a fresh. A new community. A new start. And now, I want to pray:

Great Redeemer and Father of all nations, I humbly come before your throne and offer my thanks and praise for all that you have done to bless us, your people. Please let me know you and be aware of your daily presence in my life. Forgive me, dear Father, when I haven't been a suitable place for your grace and name to dwell. Thank you for redeeming me from the sin that once entangled me. Guard my heart and rescue me from the deceptive lies of the evil one. In Jesus' name, and I say his prayer, Our father, who art in heaven, hallow by thy name, thy kingdom come, thy will be done, on earth as it in in heaven. Give us this day our daily bread, and forgive our trespasses, as we forgive those who trespass against us, and lead us not into temptation, but deliver us from evil, for thine is the kingdom and the power and the glory forever. Amen.

"Amen," the congregation echoed after him. When Henry lifted his head from prayer, he saw Sara smile at him.

After church, Henry skipped the coffee hour, and went right to the river. He did not expect anyone to come, but he figured maybe it would be okay. He had prayer and, he hoped, he had Sara.

She showed up first, a couple minutes after he did. She brought a blanket. They laid it on the grass and sat next to each other, finding calm in watching the river gently roll by. They didn't talk for a moment, but then Henry realized she was holding his hand.

"A week ago, I never would have expected this," Sara finally said.

"Me either."

"A week ago, I never thought that I would be falling in love with you."

Henry looked at her, and the two of them locked eyes. She smiled, and he felt like he could kiss her, but then the sound of a car came, pulling up. He didn't know the names of the people coming towards them, but he knew they were members of the church. He stood up, breaking away from Sara, to greet them. When he extended his hand they took it, and that was a good sign.

Soon, more and more people showed up. Some brought food. One brought a portable grill. It wasn't the type of baptism Henry was expecting, but he found himself helping the guy set it up and helped make burgers for everyone. A few kids brought frisbies. Some people swam in the river. Miranda and Callie even showed up and, although Miranda's stare was still uncomfortable, Henry took it as a good sign that she was there.

Eventually, after everyone had eaten, Henry took them all into the river. He instructed everyone to get into pairs, and they would do this twice, each time one person holding their partner up as he read them the prayer of baptism and helped them wash away all of their sins. The entire congregation of roughly 100 people paired up and waded into the river, and he blessed them with the same prayer he blessed Sara:

Living and Loving Father,
I praise and thank You with my heart for the liberation You
have given me from the clutches of sin and Satan. By Your
death on the Cross of Calvary, You have put my old life with its
sin and judgment to death forever, and endowed me with a
new life that is abounding with joy.
Father, I commit this Baptism Day into Your most precious
and loving hands. I believe that by Your crucifixion on the
Cross, my old self was rendered powerless and I was freed from
all sin. You were raised from the dead that I too may live a life
victorious and overcoming all evil.
Father, this day, I rededicate myself to live in You and live a
life for Your glory. I remember the day when I was baptized
and washed off all my sins. Lord, it is Your grace that I must be
counted worthy to be called Your child. Help me to keep Your
commandments. Renew my strength this day that I may be
strong in faith and increase in zeal. Preserve me for the
glorious day of Your coming. I believe Your Word which says,

"He who has begun a good work in you will complete it until the day of Jesus Christ." Let this day be the beginning. Lead me into greater spiritual depths even in the coming days. In Jesus' precious name I pray.
Amen.

At the end, most of the people continued swimming when Sara noticed another car pulling up, squeezing in between two other cars that had unevenly parked on the grass. She thought . . . but it couldn't be.

Nancy was pushing Bill toward the river before she knew it, and Sara couldn't help but smile. Her father had not left his house in a long time, and it was truly a miracle that he was strong enough to be able to at all.

"Henry," Sara said to him. "I want you to meet my father."

The two walked toward Bill. Sara introduced Henry to her parents, and Bill smiled at the pastor. "You have a beautiful daughter," Henry told him.

Bill smiled wider.

"And honestly . . ." Henry blushed a little. "I think I'm falling in love with her."

Bill struggled, but a moment later, he was able to lift his hand enough for Henry to grab it. The two men shook hands, and around then a congregation celebrated becoming even closer together.

AMBER & ABEL

MONICA MARKS

<u>Amber and Abel</u>

<u>Milan, Italy</u>

"No! No! No!" Amber cried, throwing her hands up in dismay. "How did this happen? How *could* this happen?"

The others in the hung their heads in unison, no one willing to accept the blame for the most recent catastrophe.

"Giuliana is to wear the taffeta number, Gia the silk and Corina the leather and lace. Who screwed this up? Come on, speak up. Time is money, people!"

Again, only mollified silence met the designer's question.

Amber stifled a groan, knowing that she would not get an admission from the group.

"Never mind now," she sighed. "Twenty minutes to curtain. Get the models re-dressed at once. Keep an eye on the rotation! It's simple reading! It's not that complicated!"

A chorus of "yes ma'am" filled her ears and she spun to deal with the next mishap as someone shoved a clipboard in her face.

It doesn't matter how many years I've been doing this, I have yet to see a fashion show go as planned.

It was not for lack of excruciating planning of course. Every detail had been mapped to the last second months in advance and yet inevitably, someone impetrative would call in sick or a top investor would want to bring his six grandchildren backstage. Invariably, a model vomited on the runway or a make-up artist and hair stylist got into a fist fight.

It was what kept Amber's blood pressure skyrocketing and her heart rushing in her ears.

"Amber! Amber, you have an urgent phone call!"

Her assistant, Dana appeared, holding out one of the three cell phones she carried but Amber waved her away.

Every phone call was an urgent phone call. It was an occupational hazard.

"Not now, Dana. Can't you see we're T minus nineteen minutes?"

"Amber, you need to take – "

"Dana! I am up to my ears in disasters right now. Can you please deal with whatever it is? Is that not what I pay you the big bucks for?"

For a timeless second, a hush seemed to fall over the bustling backstage and inexplicably, Amber felt the hairs on her arms raise as she lifted her head.

She looked at Dana who shook her head quietly.

"What is it?" Amber breathed. "What happened?"

Dana visibly swallowed, lowering her kind, brown eyes through the lenses of her glasses.

She extended the phone further.

"It's your mother."

And Amber's world stopped.

<u>Brooklyn, New York</u>

"I'm looking for Leah Colville," Amber told the nurse. She drummed her fingers anxiously on the counter as the woman punched in the information and nodded.

"Room 717," she announced. "Just follow that hallway to the end."

Amber barely heard the last words as she flew down toward her mother's room.

It was slightly ajar and she pushed it open, her stomach flipping nervously.

"Mama?" she called softly. "Mama, are you awake?"

"Amber?"

She hurried inside the semi-private room, sliding the separating curtain aside.

Leah was the only one in the room but Amber knew that could change at the drop of a hat.

Oh mama, why didn't you say anything?

Her breath caught in her throat as she stared at her one virile mother, sunken in the bed, her face as white as the sterile sheets in which she lay.

Amber threw herself into her mother's arms gently.

"Oh mama," she whispered. "Why didn't you tell me it had gotten so bad?"

Leah made a dismissive sound with her tongue.

"You are a busy girl, Amber. The last thing you need is your old, sick mom crying in your ear about chemo treatments and hair loss. It's nothing you haven't heard a million times before."

Tears filled Amber's grey eyes but she hid them.

"I am never too busy for you," she scolded tenderly. "How long have you been like this?"

Leah sighed.

"Three weeks. The doctors are shocked I've hung on this long, kitten. It's only a matter of time..."

A stunning bolt of guilt almost brought Amber to her knees.

How could I not have known for three weeks? What kind of daughter am I?

"Don't talk like that!" Amber cried. "You're not going to..."

She trailed off as her voice caught in her throat.

"Shh, kitten. Don't cry now. We have both known that I have been living on borrowed time for a long while. God has been gracious enough to let me see you become successful and now I can go to the other side knowing you are secure."

Amber pursed her lips together, squeezing her mom's frail body.

"But I need you to do something for me," the older Colville woman continued and Amber raised her head.

"Anything, mama. Tell me what you need."

Leah studied her beautiful daughter's face for a long moment, reaching up to stroke her short, layered hair.

"Two things actually."

Amber stared at her expectantly.

"First, when I die, I need you to go to Pennsylvania and find my sister, Ruthie to let her know I've passed."

Amber stared at her uncomprehendingly.

"Your sister Ruthie?" she echoed. "Since when do you have a sister Ruthie?"

Leah offered her a weak smile.

"I have always had a sister, kitten."

Amber waited for her to elaborate but Leah seemed to have lost her strength suddenly.

"I'm tired, Amber," she murmured. "I would like to rest now."

"Yes, mama, of course," Amber replied, sitting up. "I will be right here when you wake up."

Leah patted her daughter's hand and smiled lovingly.

"The second thing I would like you to do it grow your hair long again. I miss those golden locks of yours."

Amber forced a smile through the tears in her eyes.

"I will do that mama. I will grow my hair and find Aunt Ruthie in Pennsylvania."

Leah nodded slowly, her eyes growing heavy.

"Just Ruthie, not Aunt Ruthie. You can find her in Eden, Pennsylvania. Ruthie Miller."

Amber watched with a trembling chin as her mother's eyes fell closed knowing that it was the last time she would ever see them open again.

Eden, Pennsylvania

Amber looked at the woman embarrassed.

"I'm afraid I don't know much more than what I've already told you," Amber admitted, wishing away the clerk's scornful scrutiny. "My mother asked me to find her sister here in Eden and I have no idea where to start."

The clerk gave her a look which was half bemused, half annoyed but she turned back to her computer.

"Ruth Miller," she sighed, shaking her head. "There has to be at least two dozen here and that's only the ones we have one record."

Amber blinked and stared at her.

"This is city hall, isn't it? Why wouldn't you have them on record? Do you have a lot of illegal immigrants here?"

Amber's question was sincere but the clerk's expression turned sardonic.

"You really are not from around here, are you?"

Amber swallowed her annoyance and forced a smile.

"No, ma'am. I am not. That is why any help you can give me would be greatly appreciated. Why would you not have someone on record?"

"This is Amish country, honey."

Amber suddenly felt foolish and she grinned sheepishly.

"Of course. Well, can you see if any of the Ruth Millers you have there have a sister named Leah?"

The clerk's red eyebrows rose almost to her hairline.

"Ruth and Leah Miller? Are you kidding me? You're definitely looking for an Amish family, sweetie."

"That can't be," Amber said shaking her head. "My mom wasn't Amish."

"Well, I can check but if it quacks like a duck..."

Again, her fingers flew over the keyboard and she raised an eyebrow.

"I have two Ruth Millers with a sibling named Leah."

She scrawled their telephone numbers onto a piece of paper for her.

"But I wouldn't get your hopes up, honey," the clerk told her as she held out the sheet. "My guess is that your Ruth Miller is somewhere in the countryside."

Amber stared at her helplessly.

"What do I do then?"

"If neither of these women is who you're seeking, I would start combing the districts."

Amber opened her mouth to ask what that meant but the older woman seemed irritated enough.

She closed her mouth and vowed to find someone else to help her find answers.

Instead, she thanked her and hurried out of the building, into the windy autumn day.

As she stood on the steps, looking down at the phone numbers in her hands, a memory flittered through her mind.

She had been about four years old and her mother pulled a long dress from a hope chest at the foot of the bed.

It had been just after Amber's father had died and Leah had been so melancholic, digging through old photos and keepsakes.

"That's an old dress, mama," Amber said, looking at the homespun fabric in awe.

"It is, kitten, yes," her mother agreed. "Would you like to try it on?"

"Yes please!" Amber cried and Leah had laughed, slipping the too large garment onto her small daughter.

The older Colville dug into the chest and removed a small white cap, placing it on the base of Amber's head.

"You look like a proper Amish girl now, *Liebchen*."

"What is an Amish girl, mama?"

"Greta!"

The voice was loud and almost directly in her ear, smashing her reverie into a million pieces.

Startled, Amber turned to look.

An Amish man stood behind her, his green eyes alight with hope as she met his stare.

"Greta, you've returned!" he said excitedly. "When did you come back to Eden?"

Amber shook her head.

"I'm sorry," she said kindly, still awed by the green of his irises. "You have me confused with someone else."

To her surprise, his brow furrowed and he scowled slightly.

"Are you playing a game?" he asked gruffly, his eyes narrowing. "You don't need to worry; I won't tell anyone I have seen you."

Amber's eyes widened and she wondered if she was in the middle of a gag.

She looked around for cameras but nothing seemed out of the ordinary.

"I really am sorry," she said again, continuing down the steps. "You have me mixed up with someone else. My name isn't Greta."

She hurried away before he could respond, leaving him staring after her.

As she made her way toward the street where her rental car waited, she glanced back uneasily at the attractive man, her heart racing.

That was strange, she thought, sliding into the driver's side.

But as she pulled away from the curb, she wondered if it was less strange and more fate.

Perhaps that man was God's way of telling her that she would find her long lost aunt inside the Amish community after all.

I guess it's time to start combing the districts, Amber thought wryly. *Whatever that means.*

She could not help but take one last peek at the man in her rear-view as she drove away. He remained standing on the steps, staring after her as if he expected her to return.

I hope he finds Greta, she thought wistfully. *He certainly seems to love her.*

"Abel, who was that?" Levi demanded, rushing up the steps of city hall to meet his brother. He peered in the direction which the car gone.

"Apparently no one," Abel muttered as he watched the small sports car zoom away from the center of town.

"From where I stood, it looked to be Greta Shetler and – "

"It was not," Abel snapped, cutting off his brother before another word could leave his lips.

Levi eyed him warily.

"You seem upset," he commented. "Hasn't that woman done enough damage to you without having you pine for her?"

"Let's not speak about her," Abel said between clenched teeth as he hurried down the steps. "We have errands to run."

Levi chuckled dryly.

"Well whoever she is, I would not mind seeing her again," Levi commented. Abel paused to give his brother a scathing look.

"She is an Englisher," he retorted. "You would do well to stay away from her."

"Why? Are you interested?" Levi mocked. "And I thought you were going to die longing for the shunned and shamed beauty of the district."

"You are speaking nonsense now, Levi," Abel chided. "If you can't speak normally, don't speak at all."

Abel didn't have to look over to know his brother was leering at him.

It seemed everyone in town had been ogling him since the day Greta had run off with the Englisher, leaving him at the altar after declaring she was pregnant with the Englisher's child.

And now she was back, pretending that she did not recognize him.

It was just another slap in the face after her ex-communication, almost two years earlier.

Has she come back to humiliate me further?

"Who was she if not Greta?" Levi demanded, obviously unwilling to leave the topic alone.

"You know you should not even be speaking her name," Abel snapped. "I don't know who that woman was."

"Then why did you run after her if you don't know her?"

Abel was growing angry with his brother's interrogation.

"Let us go our own way today. We can accomplish more that way."

Without permitting Levi an opportunity to answer, he rushed away, trying to leave his brother in his wake along with the painful memories of Greta.

After finding a quiet spot to park her car, Amber picked up her cell phone.

She tried both the phone numbers given to her by the clerk at city hall but as the woman had predicted, neither was the woman Amber sought.

Now I have to venture from district to district, she realized. She was not looking forward to the task; it seemed daunting but she knew she could not rest until she had honored her mother's wishes.

Instinctively, she reached up and touched her hair.

It had already begun to grow out some in the two months since Leah's passing and Amber was determined not to touch it.

As she drove the rental into the outskirts of Eden, the lush Pennsylvania hills fell into a smaller settlement of land and soon, she could see that she was inside the Amish district.

Almost immediately, a feeling of peace overcame her and she had to stop the car to admire the almost surreal beauty of the landscape around her.

She grabbed for her cell phone, snapping pictures as the horizon as the sun began to set over the lolling dales.

Suddenly, she heard the clopping of hooves as a wagon approached and Amber lowered her camera, watching in awe as a horse and cart ambled toward her.

In the front, a man and woman dressed in traditional Amish attire rode primly and Amber offered them a nervous smile, not knowing if she would be received with distain.

To her relief, they both returned her beam and the man slowed the beast.

"Are you lost, miss?" he asked politely and Amber shook her head.

"No...well maybe," she replied sheepishly. "I stopped to take a picture of the beautiful landscape but..."

She trailed off, suddenly embarrassed.

"I am afraid I'm on a bit of a wild goose chase," she confessed. They peered at her with curious eyes.

"Are you looking for someone's home?" the woman asked. "Perhaps we can direct you."

Amber opened her mouth to answer and then closed it.

"This is going to seem ridiculous," she muttered. "But I am looking for a woman named Ruthie Miller. Do you know her?"

The couple seemed slightly amused by the question and Amber was beginning to realize that was going to be a common response to her inquiry.

I wonder what it would be like to live in a place where everyone knew everyone else? I imagine there is a sense of security that accompanies that knowledge.

"I fear that we know several women by that name, miss. Can you tell us anything else about her?"

"She had a sister named Leah but they have been estranged for – "

Suddenly, Amber found it difficult to speak and she swallowed quickly as her voice broke.

"Have you had supper, miss?" the woman asked quietly. "Our farm is not far from here. It would be our pleasure to have you as our guest."

Amber looked up, terrified and shook her head.

"Oh no, I couldn't," she gulped. "But thank you."

The man smiled.

"It is considered very rude to refuse a supper invitation in Amish country," he informed her and Amber could see he was teasing her but all the same, she found herself nodding.

"That would be lovely," she breathed. "Thank you."

"You may follow us," the woman said, smiling.

Amber nodded and allowed them to pass before jumping back into her car.

What lovely people, she thought, her heart warming. The man on the steps of city hall had made her nervous and so far, he had been the only interaction she had with anyone in their culture.

But he did have lovely green eyes.

Amber steered the Chrysler into up the long drive of the pretty farmhouse, keeping a safe distance behind the kind strangers.

Slowly, she exited her car, suddenly aware of how strange was what she was doing.

Would I ever accept such an unexpected dinner invitation from random strangers in New York or Milan or Paris? Of course not. So why am I doing it here?

The answer was obvious; it felt right.

She was nowhere near any major city, designing clothes and fighting with stage hands or arguing with models.

It was like she had entered another world, another planet even where Amber Colville didn't exist and she was just a lost little girl, looking for the last family relation she had left in the world.

Does my Aunt Ruthie have children? Maybe I have cousins out there. Or should I say, in here.

"Come along, miss. It's growing cold without the sun shining down on us," the woman urged.

"My name is Amber," she volunteered as she was led into the house. "Amber Colville."

The wife smiled and nodded.

"That is a lovely name. I am Beth and that is my husband, Jeremiah Troyer."

"Pleased to meet you, Mr. and Mrs. Troyer," I said politely.

She smiled softly.

"We do not use such formalities here. You may call us Beth and Jeremiah," she said softly.

Amber blushed lightly and nodded.

"Only if you call me Amber," she agreed.

"Please, come and sit. Our boys should be along shortly. They have been commissioned with supper as Jeremiah and I were in town today."

"I see," she said, nodding. "But you are farmers?"

"Yes," Beth replied. "We grow wheat and barley. Our boys have recently acquired chickens but between you and I, Amber, I am rather fearful of their pecking beaks."

Amber chuckled with Jeremiah.

"There is no shame in having fears, Beth," her husband said, reassuringly. "I am certain even the English have fears."

Amber's smile broadened.

"Oh yes," she assured them. "More fears than I care to admit."

A sudden warmth flowed between them as they stood in a comfortable silence.

"Come along inside," Jeremiah said, shooing them from the foyer. "I will see about some cider. It is cooling in the shed. Abel just made a fresh batch."

"He's a good boy, our eldest," Beth murmured but Amber noticed a dark cloud cross over her eyes as if something occurred to her.

She stared at Amber, her mouth parting slightly.

"Is something wrong, Beth?" Amber asked, immediately concerned by her change of disposition.

The older woman shook her head.

"I will help Jeremiah with the cider. The barrel can be difficult to manage. Please, sit by the fire until we return."

She was gone before Amber could reply and she was abruptly filled with a small fission of alarm.

That was strange, she thought but she was ashamed of her suspicion. *Things are just done differently here than they are in the city. There's nothing strange about it.*

"*Mamm*! *Daed*?"

She turned her head as a man called out, poking his head into the sitting room where Amber had sunk into a wing chair.

He seemed to freeze as he looked at her.

"Hello," Amber volunteered. "I'm Amber Colville. Your parents have invited me for dinner."

A small smile appeared on the young man's lips and he stalked toward her, extending his hand.

"Levi Troyer," he announced. "You were in Eden today, were you not?"

Surprised, Amber nodded.

"Yes, I was at city hall, looking for information."

Levi's eyebrow raised.

"What sort of information?" he asked curiously, placing himself into the chair facing her.

Amber swallowed and shook her head.

"It's not really important," she said quickly. "I would rather not get into it right now."

Levi's blue eyes narrowed slightly.

"I can be a wonderful source of information," he told her. "If you ever feel like talking."

His meaning was unmistakable and Amber found herself amused and slightly intrigued by the forward speaking man.

"Thank you," she replied, laughing. "Perhaps after dinner. It's not a very cheerful supper conversation."

"Levi, why did you leave me alone to finish supper. I have – "

Amber turned toward the doorway again and her jaw dropped.

"Wh -what is she doing here?" the man gasped, looking accusingly at his brother. Levi jumped to his feet, grinning.

"It appears as thought *Mamm* and *Daed* have invited her over for supper. Amber, this is my brother, Abel."

Cautiously, Amber rose to her feet, unsure of how Abel would react to her as she recalled their previous encounter.

"Hello Abel," she said quietly. "Pleased to meet you."

She wasn't sure if she should extend her hand or not but she found herself once more staring into his impossibly green eyes as if hypnotized.

He did not immediately respond and Amber felt her heart sink slightly as he continued to stare at her.

"Forgive my brother," Levi interceded. Amber turned questioningly to him.

"He seems to think you look like someone he knew once a long time ago," Levi offered and Amber nodded slightly.

"I never said that," Abel grumbled but Amber felt that his gaze betrayed his words. He could not seem to pull his irises from her face as if trying to memorize every feature.

"There you are," Beth said, hurrying into the front room, a concerned expression on her face. She held out a glass for Amber.

"This is apple cider from the Bachman's orchid," she told Amber, smiling briefly. The older woman seemed to sense the tension in the room.

"I see you have met our sons, Abel and Levi," she continued as Amber accepted the cup. "What have you made for supper, boys? I am sure our guest is as hungry as your father."

"What did the doctor say, *Mamm*?" Abel asked suddenly, diverting his attention to his mother.

Beth's face turned pale and angry.

"Abel, that is hardly an appropriate question to ask before visitors. Go tend to supper," she snapped with a harshness Amber was sure was not customary.

Abel seemed contrite but he disappeared, bowing his head somewhat shamefully.

Amber felt a spark of apprehension in her stomach as she cast Beth a sidelong look.

Why did she go to the doctor? Is she ill? Does she have cancer like mama?

Amber bit on her lower lip and tried to push the image of her mother from her mind but it was more difficult than she wished.

"Are you all right, Amber?" Beth asked, her brow furrowing deeper as she watched the blonde's face crumble.

Amber tried to nod but a tear escaped her and slid down her cheek.

"I'm sorry," the younger woman told the others, quickly wiping the streak from her face. "I recently lost my mother and I was just thinking of her. Forgive me for my display."

Beth and Levi made a commiserating noise.

"Levi, go help your brother and leave the women to talk," Beth ordered. Levi rose without protest, leaving them alone in the front room.

"It is difficult to lose a parent," Beth said comfortingly. "I have lost both of mine."

Amber sighed.

"I am so sorry, Beth. My father also died when I was very young."

Beth leaned down to pat her hand soothingly and Amber found the gesture heartwarming.

I am a perfect stranger to her and yet she feels the need to comfort me. This place is like a television program. This isn't real life. This is a place where daughters would know that their mothers have been dying for weeks, not off running fashion shows in Italy.

"Supper is ready, *Mamm*, Amber," Levi called from the dining room and the women rose to join the others at the dinner table.

"We pray before eating, Amber. You are not required to join us," Jeremiah told her as she took a seat across from the Troyer brothers.

"I would be happy to join in your prayer if you'll have me," Amber replied. She pretended not to notice the look of appreciation shared by the family as she hung her head.

Jeremiah lead the prayer in Pennsylvania Dutch but Amber could catch some of the key words from the time she had spent in Munich.

"You still have not told us what you are doing in our district, Gre – ah, Amber," Levi piped up after they had loaded their plates with meat, vegetables, potatoes and bread.

Beth and Jeremiah looked up sharply while Abel's jaw tightened.

"Were you going to call me Greta also?" Amber asked, her eyes widening. Levi seemed embarrassed.

"You do bear an uncanny resemblance to her," he confessed.

"I did not notice," Beth interjected, eyeing her older son.

"Nor did I!" Jeremiah agreed and there was a finality in his tone. It was clear that the subject was to be dropped and Amber did not want to push the issue.

Nevertheless, she was fascinated by the fact she might have an Amish twin.

"I have come here looking for my mother's sister but I'm afraid I don't have much to go off. I don't even know if I'm looking in the right spot but my mom only told me about her before she died."

Beth looked up and smiled.

"We told Amber we would happily help her find her aunt but we would need to narrow the search somehow."

"What is her name?"

Amber was surprised it was Abel who asked the question.

"Ruthie Miller. Her sister, my mother, was Leah."

The table fell silent as the family appeared to rake their memories.

"Well, I can think of four women by that name. One is far too young to be your aunt, one is much too old and the other two have lived in the district all their lives without a sister named Leah," Jeremiah volunteered, chewing his fried steak pensively. "Have I forgotten someone?"

"No...I do not believe you have," Beth replied. She gazed at her boys.

"Any suggestions?"

Levi shrugged his shoulders.

"As Amber has said, there is no guarantee that this Ruthie Miller is from this district. Perhaps I could take her to the neighboring districts tomorrow and we could investigate further."

He beamed at her and Amber smiled back but she could not help her gaze from falling on the older Troyer brother.

He seemed to glower into his plate, unspeaking.

"That would be lovely," Amber said reluctantly, realizing that Abel was not about to volunteer his help.

Is he always so brooding or is it because I remind him of this Greta?

"It's settled then. Tomorrow I will take you in search of your aunt!" Levi said jovially.

Amber could not help but notice that he gently jabbed his brother in the ribs and she wondered if she hadn't put herself in the middle of a sibling rivalry.

Abel could not sleep and he lay on his back, arms folded across his chest.

"I can feel you breathing fire over there, Abe," Levi called mockingly through the dark. "Why are you so upset?"

"I'm not!" Abel denied but Levi only laughed.

"Why don't you just admit that you want to take Amber on her search tomorrow?"

"I do not," he replied hotly but as he said the words, he knew they were a lie.

He couldn't seem to get over the remarkable likeness Amber shared to Greta. It was as if *Gotte* had sent him a chance to get things right with Greta.

That's ridiculous. They are two different women. If Levi wishes to waste his time with an Englisher, let him do it.

"You truly are a fool," Levi sighed, sitting up. Abel turned his head to scowl at his brother in the moonlit room.

"You would know a fool to see one, brother," he snapped. "Stop talking and let me go to sleep."

Levi groaned.

"I only offered to take Amber tomorrow because I knew you wouldn't. You will pick her up at her hotel in Eden and take her."

"I will not!" Abel was insulted at the idea of stealing his brother's date. "She has agreed to go with you, not me."

"But she wants to go with you," Levi insisted. "She could not stop staring at you all through dinner. Didn't you notice?"

Abel had not.

"Of course you didn't notice. You were too busy sulking about Greta to notice the lovely woman yearning for you to look at her. I think Amber is *Gotte's* way of telling you that it is time to move on."

"What do you know?" Abel growled but in his heart, he felt a sliver of hope.

Is he just telling me that because he believes I have spent too much time pining over Greta or did Amber find me interesting?

"I know that if you don't act on this opportunity, I will give you no more second chances. I will pursue Amber myself."

Abel didn't answer but his heart sank at his brother's words.

Maybe this is a sign from Gotte. What harm can it do to take her tomorrow?

Amber felt a spark of happiness when she saw Abel at the reins the following morning in front of the Eden Resort and Suites.

"I hope you do not mind that I have come in my brother's place," Abel said, somewhat gruffly but Amber was already learning that it was shyness, not rudeness.

"I am very happy it was you," she replied earnestly, catching his eye.

A shiver coursed down her spine as he helped her onto the wagon and they made their way out of town toward the districts.

She found herself studying his handsome profile, taking in the fine shape of his nose and delicate bone structure.

"I hope that you will not be disappointed," Abel told her as they started their ride in silence.

Amber glanced at him in surprise, thinking that he had caught her staring at him.

She blushed and shook her head.

"I'm not disappointed in the least," she replied, lowering her eyes.

He shot her a sidelong look and gave her a lopsided smile.

"I meant that I hope you find your aunt," he explained. Amber turned bright red and cleared her throat in nervousness.

"Of course," she muttered, doubly ashamed.

She had almost forgotten the reason for their drive as if they were merely on a date.

Focus on the task at hand, she told herself.

Soon, they were in one of the neighboring districts and Abel proved to be a wonderful guide, finding a minister to question almost immediately.

They did not find anyone to match their description in the first two districts they visited but as they made their way into the third, it was growing late in the afternoon and Amber was growing disheartened.

"I'm beginning to think this is a lost cause," Amber confessed as they searched for the home of the deacon as directed by a young girl playing hopscotch.

Despite her mounting disappointment, she could not shake the idyllic beauty of their community.

I would give it all up to live here, she thought as they found Deacon Roth tending to his herb garden.

"Hello, Deacon," Abel called. "I am Abel Troyer and this is my friend, Amber. We have some questions for you if you have a moment."

The deacon looked up and nodded, smiling welcomingly.

"Of course," he agreed. "What can I help you with?"

"Deacon, have you a Ruthie Miller who lives here? She would be in her forties or fifties with an estranged sister named Leah?"

The elderly man's mouth parted and he stared at Amber for a long moment.

"Indeed," he murmured. "Are you Ruthie's daughter?"

Amber shook her head.

"No...I am Leah's daughter," Amber replied, glancing nervously at Abel. "Do you know them?"

The man nodded thoughtfully.

"Of course, I remember Leah. She never was baptized. She fell in love with an Englisher and married him when she was nineteen or so."

Amber nodded excitedly.

"Yes! Alexander Colville. That was my father," Amber gushed. "Is Ruthie still here?"

"No, child. Ruthie was married to a man named Samuel Miller but he died in a terrible accident not two years after the wedding. That was about a year after Leah had left the district."

Amber found her palms sweating and she wiped them on her jeans.

"Where did she go? Did my aunt leave the community too?"

The deacon chuckled.

"No, no. She eventually remarried and moved on to another district."

"Nearby?" Amber pressed, her excitement mounting.

I'm so close to finding your sister, mama! She thought, her heart racing.

"Yes, two districts across."

Abel's face turned confused.

"Closest to Eden?" he asked and the older man nodded.

"But that's our district," Abel murmured. A look of understanding crossed his face.

"Who did she marry when she moved?" he asked.

The deacon thought for a long moment, digging into the depth of his swiss cheese memory bank.

"Ah yes. David Shetler. As far as I know, they still live there but I confess, I am out of touch sometimes," Deacon Roth chortled.

Abel's face turned grey.

"Do you know these people, Abel?" Amber asked excitedly. "Do you know where I can find them?"

He looked at her, his face aghast.

"Yes," he whispered. "I know them. They are Greta's parents. You are Greta's cousin."

The ride back to Eden was long and quiet as Abel tried to gather his thoughts. To his relief, Amber did not push him to speak as if she could sense he needed the quiet.

Is this a cruel joke? Sending me a cousin of the woman who broke my heart? One who looks so much like her?

But as they continued the journey back, Abel suddenly realized that he had been blinded by Amber's outward appearance.

True, she looked like Greta with the solemn grey eyes as sunny blonde hair but how similar were the two really?

Greta could not seem to run away fast enough, sacrificing her own values to do so while Amber embraced her mother's home and heritage in tribute.

Greta was selfish and hurtful while Amber was kind and loving.

Greta was gone and Amber was right there beside him, waiting for him to speak, to make the next step.

"It is getting late," he finally told her. "I don't think it is wise to interrupt your aunt at this hour although I am certain she will be happy to see you, regardless of the time."

Amber nodded but he could see the sadness in her eyes.

"That's fine. I can find my own way there tomorrow," she replied, trying to sound cheerful. "But I appreciate all your help."

She turned her head quickly but he knew it was only so he wouldn't see the tears in her eyes.

He paused, searching for the next words to say.

Opening his mouth, his perfectly concocted statement flew into the air.

"I am hungry," he said instead.

Amber turned to glance at him.

"You're hungry?" she repeated. "Oh."

She wasn't quite sure what to make of the statement.

"Me too," she replied suddenly.

Their eyes met and they smiled.

"May I buy you dinner, Amber?" he asked her sweetly.

"Like a date?" she teased.

His smiled faded and he nodded solemnly.

"Exactly like a date," he replied.

END

LOVINA'S HEART

DEIDRA SCOTT

Chapter One

Lovina Miller took a deep breath as she reached up to pull a piece of laundry from the clothesline and put it in the basket at her feet. Above her head, a pair of bluebirds danced through the bright June sky, reminding her that summer was quickly approaching.

Summer. It was a time full of fresh starts and new beginnings.

Looking across the yard, Lovina watched David Yoder working with one of her brothers. Together, the two young men were struggling with their task, trying to break her *daed's* new horse.

Ach, just watching David sent a thrill of excitement through Lovina's heart. Although she had known him most of her life, there was something about him that could still put a spark inside of her, giving her the feeling that they had just met.

Growing up, Lovina had always dreamed of marrying David. It had just seemed natural to her. With their two houses located side-by-side, they had spent all of their childhood hours playing together in the creek that wound between their properties and climbing the big apple tree like little monkeys.

Lovina had decided early on that she and David would grow old together, spending their adult days raising babies and making a life within their Amish community.

Now that Lovina had turned eighteen-years-old, she felt like she was stuck in the midst of a waiting game, simply counting down the hours until David came forward to begin their relationship together.

Smiling to herself, Lovina basked in the realization that, as an adult, it was now time to watch her childhood dreams start to unfold.

"Danki for the help, David!" Lovina heard her father call out from the barn and looked up in time to see David waving goodbye to her family as he started across the yard.

Lovina felt her heart go aflutter when, rather than take the path back to his own parents' house, David veered closer to her own home and made a bee-line right for the clothesline where she was working.

"*Gut* afternoon, David!" Lovina called out, her voice seeming somewhat weak to her own ears.

Watching him come closer, Lovina couldn't help but marvel at how handsome her childhood friend had become. With a head-full of dark red hair and sparkling blue eyes, David had always looked like a cheerful storybook character; however, as he aged, he grew tall and muscular, his boyish looks transforming into that of a good-looking man.

"Hello there, Lovina," David called back, rolling down his sleeves as he walked along, "I tell you, that horse of your *daed's* nearly got me down this time!"

Lovina smiled as she pulled a pair of her brother's pants off of the laundry line and tossed them in the basket, "I guess we should consider ourselves glad to have such a good horse-breaker living so near-by."

To her surprise, David's face suddenly seemed to darken. Taking a deep breath, he reached up and put one hand on the clothesline, "Actually, Lovina, I wanted to talk to you about that."

Although Lovina had hoped that David would want to talk to her alone, she could already tell that his news wasn't going to be what she had wanted to hear.

"Lovina," David looked out across the fields, "Ever since you had your birthday, I'd been hoping..." his voice trailed off and he gave a shrug, "Well, nothing I'd hoped for is going to work out this summer." Standing up taller, he announced, "My uncle from Indiana wrote telling about the need for a good horse-trainer in his community. I agreed to go help for the next three months...I'll be home in time to help my dad get started on the harvest."

Lovina felt her heart drop in her chest. The idea that David would leave had never entered her mind. Even though it was only for three months, it felt like it might as well be three years.

"*Ach*, Lovina, don't be so sad," David reached out and placed his hand on her arm, "I'll be back – I promise. Kentucky is my home...I sure don't have any plans to run off for good."

Something about having his hand on her arm made the pain a little more bearable. Looking up, Lovina met David's tender gaze with her own.

"When I come back..." David took a deep breath and kicked at a clump of grass with his foot. It was strange to see him so uncomfortable – David was usually one to be bold and daring, willing to say whatever was necessary.

"When I come back, I hope we can spend more time together," David managed to say, "Seems like we've grown apart over the years, and I'm ready for that to end."

Lovina couldn't stop the smile that spread across her face, "And maybe not be climbing trees this time?" She added.

David laughed, "Of course we'll be climbing trees again!" He teased.

Growing more sober, he lifted his hand and ran it gently across her cheek, "I'll see you in three months, 'Vina."

Three months. As she watched him walk away and back to his parents' farm across the creek, Lovina took a deep breath and tried to still her thumping heart. Three months was a long time – she was just glad that she had those tender moments to cling to during the summer that stretched out before her.

Chapter Two

Taking a deep breath, David watched out the passenger window as the driver he had hired took him farther and farther from his home in Kentucky and on toward his Uncle Amos' house in Indiana.

"Are you nervous about leaving home for so long?" David's paid driver, Mr. Simpson asked, as he flipped his turn signal on and proceeded toward Uncle Amos' house.

David shook his head and laughed, "*Ach*, no, not nervous."

"Anxious to get away from your parents?" Mr. Simpson asked with a chuckle.

"No, nothing like that." David assured him, "Just glad to be helping my uncle and the people in his community."

Leaning his head back against the headrest of the seat, David closed his eyes and thought about Mr. Simpson's question.

Was he glad to be getting away from his parents? Although he had been quick to assure his driver that wasn't he case, David wasn't so certain himself. To be completely honest, David wasn't a bit sorry to be leaving for the summer. While he had always loved his home and his family, David relished the chance to get away.

Since David had been a little boy, he had always known what was expected of him. He was going to settle down, buy a piece of property close to his parents, and marry Lovina Miller. It wasn't a bad plan at all, but it seemed so boring and dull. Deep in his heart, David had always dreamed of excitement and adventure. Maybe his trip to Indiana would finally provide him with a chance to enjoy his freedom before he settled down for good.

David's driver took him straight to Uncle Amos' house, helped him unload his bags, and then left him to head back to Kentucky.

Uncle Amos and his entire family were happy to welcome David to their home. Uncle Amos explained that everyone in the community could use his horse breaking services and that they would be bringing their horses to his house so that David could train them. Uncle Amos also said that, during David's spare time he could help the family out in the dry goods store they had located in a small shed next to the road.

"I'll take you out to the store now, so that I can show you what kind of work you can do out there." Uncle Amos suggested once David had put his clothes away in the spare bedroom.

Leading David across the yard, Uncle Amos explained, "Of course, I will pay you for helping in the store...and you can also have all the money for training the horses."

David shook his head, "*Ach,* that's too much, Uncle Amos. I'm happy to have the chance to help out."

Uncle Amos chuckled and reached out to give David a slap on the back, "Now, now, don't go talking like that. I'm sure a handsome young man like you should be saving back to buy a nice farm and making plans for the future. I'd dare say that some pretty girl back home has caught your eye."

David gave a shrug, not too anxious to think about his future, "Nothing set in stone just yet."

The graveled lane ended and the two men found themselves standing side-by-side outside of the dry goods store. Reaching out, Uncle Amos pushed the door open, revealing a building with shelves full of baking supplies, canned goods, and some craft items.

"Hannah!" Uncle Amos called out, as he led David through the small building, "Hannah!"

"I'm over here," a soft voice returned.

Turning the corner around one of the shelves, they found a young Amish woman on her knees, busy stacking bags of flour.

"Hannah, I want you to meet my nephew, David," Uncle Amos announced, "David, this is Hannah – she is my wife's cousin and she's helping us out in the store this summer."

Hannah pulled herself to her feet and turned to stare up at David with large, blue eyes. Wisps of dark hair had escaped her prayer *kapp,* making a sort of halo around her face.

Just looking at her, David felt his heart give a leap. She was so unexpectedly beautiful in a dark, mysterious way.

"*Gut* to meet you, David," Hannah replied timidly.

"David is likely to be helping out in the store when he isn't working with the horses," Uncle Amos explained. Giving David a pat on the arm, he motioned toward the back room, "Come on, I want to show you where I store the bulk supplies."

As David followed his uncle, he had a hard time even listening to what was being said. His mind was still mesmerized by the beautiful and timid young lady he had just met. David could hardly wait to get to know and learn more about Hannah.

Lovina sat on the edge of her bed, looking out across the fields of farmland through her bedroom window. Knowing that David was no longer in the house next-door left a hollow emptiness in Lovina's heart. In her eighteen-years, she had never gone a summer without seeing David.

Lovina tired to imagine what her sweet friend was doing at that moment. Did he realize how much she was thinking of him? Did he miss her at all?

Lovina closed her eyes and took a deep breath, "Dear God," she whispered into the darkness, "Please, bring the man that I love back to me."

Chapter Three

David carefully guided his uncle's buggy down the road. It was only his second day in Indiana and work was already starting to pick up; however, Uncle Amos had sent him to town to pick up some nails for a woodworking project he was doing in the barn.

The summer afternoon sun shone down on David and the warmth of the breeze put a smile on his face. David was enjoying his time away from home and, although he had not had many opportunities to spend time with Hannah, he had hopes that would change eventually.

The buggy suddenly took a lung, pulling David out of his thoughts.

"Woah, boy! Woah!" David pulled tightly on the reigns, unsure of what was happening to the buggy. Carefully guiding the horse to the side of the road, he jumped down from his seat and looked over the situation.

Something was wrong with the front buggy wheel. Grabbing a hold of it, David gave it a wiggle, trying to determine if it could keep going.

Pulling off his straw hat, David slapped it against his leg in frustration. He couldn't get to town on that wheel and he didn't think he could make it back to his uncle's house either.

The clipping of oncoming horse hooves made David stand up straighter and wave desperately at the approaching buggy.

The driver was a single Amish man. As soon as David caught his attention, the other driver pulled his buggy to the side of the road behind David.

"Hi there!" David greeted with a smile as he watched the other Amish man get off his buggy and start toward him, "Boy, I sure am glad to see you!" Sticking out a hand, he announced, "I'm David Yoder. I'm staying with my Uncle Amos Yoder – you probably know him."

The stranger nodded and simply said, "I'm Luke Christner." Taking a deep breath, he walked over to the buggy and squatted down to inspect the wheel.

"Looks like this is busted good," he announced, pushing his hat back on his head and reaching up to wipe some sweat from his brow.

David groaned, "I was afraid of that."

Standing to his feet, Luke continued, "I'm afraid you shouldn't drive it any farther than just a few feet or you'll end up wrecking or destroying your entire buggy." With a slight smirk, Luke added, "Lucky for you, this is my parents' drive right up ahead. And I just happen to work on buggies for a living."

David's eyes got large and he let out a huge sigh, "Oh, *gut*! Do you think that you could help me out?"

Luke nodded, "Sure thing. Just lead your buggy down to my workshop. I'll have her fixed up in just a bit."

True to his word, Luke had the buggy wheel fixed within an hour.

David stayed by the young man who had rescued him and worked to fill him in on all the details about his life, his home, and his family. Luke, who seemed to be more reserved, was happy to listen and donate very few details of his own.

"How much do I owe you?" David asked as Luke put the repaired wheel back on his buggy.

Luke gave a shrug as he secured the wheel in place, "Nothing. Consider it a welcome present. Maybe you can help me with one of my horses one day this summer."

"*Ach*," David raised an eyebrow, "I can't let you do that. I took some time you could have been working on other projects..."

Before he could finished, Luke started shaking his head, "No, no you didn't," he assured David as he stood up straight, "Honestly, I didn't have any other work for today." Sighing deeply, he announced, "As badly as we need a horse trainer in this area, we do not need any kind of buggy work. Jobs around here are scarce, David. I was glad to help."

David pondered Luke's statement for a moment. As an idea entered his mind, a broad smile spread across his face, "Listen, Luke! You may not be needed here, but you sure would be in my community! How would you feel about going to Kentucky to spend the summer with my family? It would sure help them out while I'm gone, and you could earn money doing buggy repairs and carpentry work!"

Luke was silent, obviously studying David's suggestion. Finally, with a shrug, he announced, "*Jah* – I don't see why that wouldn't be great. *Danki*, David."

The entire plan made David's face light up like that of a little boy. Grinning from ear-to-ear, he grabbed his new friend's hand in a shake and started making plans to get Luke back to Kentucky.

Chapter Four

Lovina reached up to wipe some sweat from her forehead as she took a break from chopping weeds out of the row of green beans. Despite all her hard work, the weeds were quickly starting to overtake the plants.

David had now been gone two weeks, and Lovina had yet to hear anything from him. His absence made her sad and she wished for all she was worth that she would receive a letter.

Glancing across the field toward his house, she thought of all the times they had snuck away from their chores and played together instead.

To her surprise, Lovina saw a young man approaching her. Could it be...? Lovina's heart dropped as he drew closer. Although she had hoped that it was David, she instantly realized that her eyes had been playing tricks on her. This stranger was even taller than her dear childhood friend and slightly thinner.

"Hullo," Lovina called out as he continued to draw closer.

"Hullo," the stranger returned, his voice deep and almost mysterious, "Are you Lovina Miller?"

Lovina stood up straighter and adjusted her prayer *kapp*, "That would be me. Do I know you?"

The stranger shook his head, "No, you don't." Now he was so close that Lovina was able to get a good look at him. This strange Amish man looked to be in his early twenties, but he seemed more mature. His brown hair was so dark it was almost black, and his eyes a dark color chocolate. Just looking at him made Lovina take a deep breath of surprise. *Ach*, it was hard to remember a time that she had ever seen such a *gut*-looking man!

"I'm Luke Christner. I know your friend, David, and I'm staying with his family until he returns." Glancing toward her house, Luke asked, "Is your *daed* at home? The Yoders told me that he has a construction crew and I'd like a job."

Lovina felt so out of sorts, she wasn't sure what to do. Looking down at her bare feet, she tried to gather her composure. Taking a deep breath, she said, "*Nee*, my *daed* isn't home from work yet, but we're expecting him any minute. If you'd like to wait in the house, my *mamm* can give you some fresh lemonade and cookies."

Luke glanced from the house back to Lovina and then shrugged, "If you don't mind, I'll just stay out here. Looks like you could use some help." Grabbing for an extra hoe, Luke set to work, removing the pesky weeds from among the rows of bean plants.

There was something about Luke that made Lovina feel uncertain about everything. He was a good help in the garden, but she certainly would have felt more at-ease without him. On the other hand, she dreaded him leaving once her father got home from work. Just being near him made her feel things that she had never experienced – she found herself overwhelmed by a sort of giddiness that sprung up from deep within. Although Lovina had always been a talker, she suddenly seemed almost speechless.

"You don't have to do this," Lovina assured him.

Luke simply set his jaw and turned to look at her with his brooding, dark eyes, "I don't have to...but I want to."

Lovina felt weak in the knees, as if she might keel right over. Taking a deep breath, she tried to stead herself.

Suddenly, she found herself a little glad that David was going to be gone for the summer. As quickly as the thought flitted through her mind, she pushed it away; however, just the realization that she could think such a thing left Lovina questioning everything about the future.

David washed his hands in a pail of water that had been set out by the barn, preparing himself for the evening meal. Inside the house, Aunt Miriam was putting the finishing touches on a pot of homemade chili with the help of three of David's cousins.

True to Uncle Amos' word, in the time that David had spent in Indiana he had already been so busy, he hardly had time to even think about being at home.

Wiping his clean hands on a towel, David glanced across the acres of land that his uncle owned. There, in the glowing darkness of the evening, he could make out the form of a young woman walking near the pond.

Hannah.

David had learned to recognize her from a distance. Even though it would be hard to distinguish her from any other Amish woman from so far away, David could pick Hannah out because she was always alone. It seemed like she carried an air of sadness with her, wherever she went.

Taking a deep breath, David stepped out of the barn and started the short walk to the pond.

"Hi there," David called out as he drew near to Hannah.

The young woman looked up at him and gave a sad smile.

"What are you doing?"

Hannah gave a shrug and pulled her black shawl tighter against her shoulders, "I just felt like a walk," she explained.

David stepped up next to her side, "It must be sort of lonely to walk all alone."

Hannah shrugged again, "I'm used to being alone."

David *thought* over his childhood and how little time he had ever spent just to himself. There were always siblings to play with, other Amish children to enjoy at events, and Lovina. Lovina had always been there for him.

Just the thought of his old friend's name sent a nagging sense of guilt through his mind.

Hadn't he promised Lovina that, when he got home, things would be different? Hadn't he promised that they would spend time together? So, what was he doing, trying to get closer to Hannah?

"David..." Hannah's soft voice brought him out of his thoughts, "Are you all right, David? I've never seen you so solemn and quiet."

David looked up at her in surprise, his face breaking out in a broad grin, "Oh, *jah*, I'm fine. I was just thinking is all."

"I didn't know you were able to do that...you know, think without saying what was going through your mind." Although Hannah's words were haughty, David *looked* up in time to catch a teasing smile cross her lips. It was the first time he had ever seen her smile and, something about it made him want to see it a thousand times more.

"Maybe it's too much time around you," David suggested, "Because I don't think you ever say anything much at all."

Hannah's tender smirk turned into a broad smile and David was, once again, captivated by her charm.

Reaching out, he gently took her elbow in his hand, "Would you do me the honor of letting me walk with ya tonight?"

Hannah was silent for a moment, studying David for all that he was worth. Finally, she nodded slowly and said, "*Jah* – I suppose that might be nice."

Chapter Five

Just as David had predicted, it was easy for Luke to find work in Kentucky. He not only spent his afternoons working on buggies in the Yoder's empty shed, but also joined the carpentry work crew lead by Lovina's father.

Lovina wasn't exactly sure how it happened, but it seemed that she and Luke were constantly thrown in the paths of one another. Lovina tried to convince herself that it was merely a coincidence, but she had to admit that it was more than that.

The longer David was gone, the less she was thinking about him and the more she was thinking about Luke.

When he wasn't busy with work, Luke frequently dropped by to help Lovina in the garden; although he wasn't a talker, there was something about his calm attitude that left Lovina yearning for more time with him.

One evening, Lovina baked a plate of her famous homemade ginger snap cookies and decided to take a few across the creek as a thank you for Luke's help in the garden.

Knocking on the shed door, she cautiously pushed it open, cheerfully announcing, "Hello! Luke! Are ya in here?"

"*Jah*, I'm here," Luke replied.

There he was, standing next to a work bench with a busted buggy wheel laid out in front of him.

"Hi there!" Lovina greeted him, suddenly feeling unsure of herself and terribly bashful, "I thought I might bring you something." Placing the plate of cookies on the work table, she watched Luke eyeball them before picking one up and putting it in his mouth.

"It's just a thank you for all the help you've been giving me," she explained.

Luke raised his eyebrows and nodded as he swallowed, "*Danki* – they're very good. You're a good baker, Lovina."

Lovina felt her heart skip a beat with his compliment. Looking at the work he was doing, she added, "Looks like you've got quite a few talents of your own."

Reaching for another cookie, Luke gave a shrug, "I keep busy for sure....but that's a good thing. I'm always thankful for the money."

Leaning back against the table, Lovina studied him in the growing darkness, "Saving back for a farm of your own?"

Luke stared straight at his work and shook his head, "No. I'm going to give my money to help out my family. I have no need of a place of my own."

"Don't you ever hope to get married and have a family?"

Luke shook his head slowly, "I'm afraid all of my dreams are gone. I plan to be alone forever."

His words broke Lovina's heart. Although he tried to sound resolved, it was easy to hear the pain in his voice.

"*Ach*, Luke," she managed to whisper with a smile, "Don't say that. You never know what might happen."

Luke took in a deep breath and then let it out slowly. Looking up to meet Lovina's eyes, he studied her for what seemed minutes before asking, "What about you? Do you think that you could ever love someone like me?"

His question took Lovina by such surprise that she almost fell over. Her eyes growing large, she looked down at the floor, her heart flooded by a million different emotions.

"I...I...Luke..." Lovina's voice was trailing in every direction but her words were making no sense at all.

"Lovina," Reaching out, Luke put his hand on top of hers, "Would you consider going with me to the singing after church this weekend?"

It felt like Lovina would not be able to breath, so many decisions were running helter-skelter through her mind. Almost a surprise to herself, she heard her voice say, "Sure. I don't see why not."

Although David had been staying busy with the horses, he still managed to make some time to help out in the store. With a beautiful girl like Hannah there, he had to find time to spend with her.

One afternoon they had received a large order of supplies and were hurrying to put them on the shelves before it would be too dark to see, even by the glow of the lantern.

"*Ach*, this is a job!" David grumbled as he hurried to put some bags of flour in their place on a shelf, "Of course this would just happen to be the night that Uncle Amos and his entire family went visiting...leaving you and me to do all the work."

Hannah smiled and shook her head, "David, you complain so much. I don't mind the work. Work keeps me busy...work keeps my mind off of...other things."

Suddenly interested, David looked up in surprise. Maybe he would finally have a chance to hear some of the secrets that were hidden away behind this mysterious girl's sad blue eyes.

"What other things?" David asked.

Hannah shrugged as she ran her fingers over a bag of sugar, "Disappointments...heartbreaks...bad decisions."

Hannah went silent, assuring David that he would hear no more of her story, but then she surprised him when she went on to clear her throat and say, "I had a boyfriend...a fiancé even."

As the words came pouring out of her mouth, it was easy to see that they were tearing her apart. Hannah closed her eyes and continued, "But things didn't work out. We were engaged but...well, I was filled with so many uncertainties. I called off the wedding before it was even announced in church. I didn't mean to end everything with him – I just needed more time to think. But I'm afraid he took it as an outright rejection. And now, I'll never have a chance with him again," Hannah reached up to wipe away the tears that were threatening to overwhelm her, "*Ach*, David, it almost breaks my heart to talk about it. I have destroyed all my chances for happiness."

Looking at her in the light of the lantern, her face clouded over with pain and tears gathering in her eyes, David felt totally broken for her. Pulling himself to his feet, he stood up straight and stepped closer to her, putting a hand on her thin shoulder.

"Hannah," he whispered her name with all the tenderness that he had been storing in his heart, "Dear Hannah...you still have a thousand chances for happiness." Reaching up, he took his thumb and brushed a tear off of her cheek.

Hannah took a deep breath and let it out slowly. Looking at him in surprise, she simply whispered, "*Danki*, David." Then she squared her shoulders and announced, "Let's get back to work."

Chapter Six

Over the next few days, David and Hannah had little time to spend together. He looked forward to ever chance he had to see her. Although their friendship had not had time to progress, David felt confident that over the rest of the summer he could easily earn himself a special place in Hannah's lonely heart.

One afternoon, David had finally found a chance to work in the dry goods store alongside Hannah when one of his cousins came rushing into the shed with a letter in his outstretched hand.

"David," the little cousin called out, "You got some mail!"

Taking the letter, David quickly recognized the handwriting as that of his younger sister, Lydia.

Ripping the seal open, David pulled out the letter, unsure why his teenage sister would even take the time to write him.

Dear David,

I don't want to bother you while you're gone, but I need to let you know something important. I've always thought that you and Lovina had something special together, although I'm not sure if you had any kind of plans for the future or an agreement. While you've been gone, Lovina has taken a spark to the very man you sent here to work – Luke Christner. Seems like they're seeing each other almost every day and last night I overheard him invite her to the singing Sunday night. She agreed to go with him.

I don't mean to stick my nose in where it doesn't belong, but I know that you were always sweet on Lovina and just thought you should know.

Your sister,

Lydia

"*Ach,*" David read over the letter and then reread it again, his heart suddenly dropping into his stomach.

Lovina – with Luke? A multitude of emotions suddenly assailed David. He found himself so frustrated, almost angry at Luke for stealing his girl. How dare Luke go to David's own home and try to take the woman he loved away from him? David was hurt, so hurt, by Lovina's decision to move forward with a relationship with someone else. But, worst of all, David felt incredible guilt and sadness.

Deep in his heart, David realized that it was his own fault that Lovina and Luke were growing close. In all the time that David had been in Indiana, he had never taken the time to even write his childhood sweetheart a letter – he had just always taken for granted that she would be there for him when he returned.

While he had been busy pursing a friendship with Hannah, he had never thought that Lovina might be looking at someone else.

Reaching up, David rubbed his hand across his face, trying to gather his wits and decide what to do next.

"What is wrong, David?" Hannah asked softly as she stepped up next to him.

David balled his free hand up into a fist, fighting the urge to destroy the letter he had just received. Passing it to Hannah, he quickly explained, "I don't know how to tell you this, Hannah, but Lovina...well, she and I have always been friends. I don't mean to have led you astray in any way because I have liked you since the day we met but this..." David couldn't go on.

Hannah took the letter in her own hands and read it slowly, her eyes growing large as she went over the message again and again.

"David," she managed to breath softly, "What are you going to do?"

David brushed his hand through his hair as memories of Lovina ran across his mind, "I don't know. I just don't know." Turning, he gave the floor a hard kick with the toe of his boot.

"David," Hannah took a deep breath and shook her head slowly, "I hate to say this, but you know that we aren't meant to be together. No matter how happy we might have both been to pretend...it just isn't so. You have made my summer much more enjoyable...but it's time to get back to our real lives."

David looked down at his feet. He wanted to fight her words; he hated the idea of giving Hannah up completely. But, when he thought of his dear Lovina...he knew that he couldn't live without her.

"Go to her, David!" Hannah exclaimed, "Go to Lovina and let her know that you love her."

Taking a deep breath, David nodded his head, "I'll go call a driver right now."

Chapter Seven

David sat in the passenger seat of the truck, half-heartedly listening as his driver talked incessantly during the long trip back home. Looking out the window, David watched the scenery slowly change from the flat Amish country of Indiana to the rolling hills of Kentucky.

With each mile that passed, it seemed that David got even more nervous about his future with Lovina.

When he first started home, he had been certain that she would be glad to see him but now...well, the closer he got to her, the less sure he became. Maybe she had truly fallen for Luke and she wouldn't want to even see him. Maybe David had blown his one and only chance for true love with the only girl he ever truly cared for.

Lovina had just filled up a bucket of water and got down on her knees to scrub the kitchen floor with a scrub brush when she heard a truck pull up in the front yard.

Ach, Lovina thought to herself as she plunged her hands down into the soapy water, *Daed must have visitors.*

It was Saturday afternoon and Lovina found her mind plagued with thoughts of Luke and their upcoming date. Although she truly enjoyed spending time with him, there was something about agreeing to go on a date with him that put her mind entirely in a tizzy. As much as she liked Luke and was attracted to him, Lovina battled thoughts of David – it seemed so sad to be turning her back on their relationship with each other.

But, she reasoned to herself, when she thought back on it, she and David had never had a true relationship. Sure, he had always been a good friend to her, but it seemed that was all things were to ever be. Since he left for Indiana, she had not heard a word from him and, as sad as she was to admit it, she was starting to wonder if he would ever come home at all.

"Lovina."

The voice seemed to come out of no where. Lovina looked up in surprise, wondering if she was truly hearing a person or if it was her own imagination.

There, standing in the doorway to the kitchen, was David himself.

"David!" Lovina managed to breathe as she struggled to pull herself to her feet, "Oh, David...is that really you?"

In an instant, David had bridged the space between them. He came right to her side, nearly knocking her bucket of soapy water over in his hurry.

"Lovina," David managed to say, somewhat louder this time, "Lovina..." he seemed to want to say more, but acted as if he couldn't find the words. Reaching out, he grabbed Lovina and gathered her into his arms.

To Lovina, everything felt like a crazy dream. Pressed firmly against her old friend's body, all thoughts of Luke vanished from her mind as she let David hold her like a little girl.

"Lovina," David pulled back only long enough to kiss her on the mouth, "Lovina, I have been a total moron. I am so sorry!"

"David," Lovina managed to say as she tried to catch her breath, "David...what has happened?"

David stepped back as he struggled to gather his composure. Reaching up, he wiped away at tears that threatened to overtake him.

"Lovina," he reached out and held her hands in his own, "I have been so ignorant. I left home, anxious to find adventure and experience new things...and I almost lost the one thing that means the most to me in the world – you."

Lovina felt her heart start to melt as David poured out his soul to her, "Lovina, I love you. I love you more than I ever realized. I thought that Uncle Amos was giving me a chance to experience adventure but I think it was actually the good Lord allowing me the opportunity to realize how much I love you. Please, Lovina...I don't want to wait any longer. Say that you will marry me!"

There had never been anything that Lovina wanted more. In that instant, it felt like all of her hopes and dreams were finally coming true.

Luke.

The name entered her mind suddenly and it felt like the life was drained right out of her. Oh, but hadn't she already led him to believe that she cared for him? Hadn't she already agreed to go out on a date with him this very weekend?

"David," Lovina squeezed her dear friend's hands tightly as she looked for the right words to share her news, "David. I have been a foolish girl."

"And I have been a foolish man," David was quick to add.

Lovina smiled and shook her head, "Perhaps we've both been foolish..."

Her words were cut short as the sound of an approaching vehicle brought them both from their thoughts.

Glancing out the window, they watched together as a strange car stopped in front of the house and let out a passenger.

David felt his heart sink when he saw the visitor who was getting out of the strange car.

It was Hannah.

David thought that she had understood. What was she doing...following him all the way to Kentucky of all places? Hadn't she been the one who had said that their relationship wasn't going to work and even pushed him to return to Lovina? What was she doing here now?

David battled the urge to run forward and stop her before she could get to the house. Turning to Lovina, he struggled to find the words to explain what was surely about to come.

"Lovina..." he hurried to say, "While I was gone, I was an idiot. I hate telling you this more than you will ever know, but I got involved with a girl from Indiana. We never started to court, but we were heading in that direction when I heard that you and Luke had begun a relationship...."

As the words poured from his mouth, David watched Lovina's face turn ashen and then red with shame.

"You already know about Luke?" She managed to whisper.

David nodded his head, "That was the wake-up call I needed. That was what I needed to bring me back home. I never want to risk losing you again, Lovina!"

Lovina started to wipe tears away from her eyes, "David, I don't want to lose you either! But what you heard is true. Luke and I have grown close and are on the verge of starting a relationship. I was so foolish, David, but I was afraid I had lost you and now I don't know what to do..."

In the other room, they could hear a knock on the front door.

Wiping at her eyes, Lovina hurried to go open it with David trailing close behind. When she opened the door, Hannah was standing on the front porch, a determined look in her blue eyes.

"I need to talk to David," she announced, looking from Lovina to David.

"David," she took a deep breath, "I need to go to your house...I need to see Luke."

Luke? David was more confused than ever. Cocking his head to one side, he tried to understand where this strange twist came into play.

"You don't have to look far," the deep voice of Luke spoke out and they all turned in surprise to find that he had come up on the porch and was standing just out of view.

"Hannah," as he said the name, his voice seemed to fill with a strange sort of pain.

"*Ach*, Luke..." Hannah looked down at her black shoes as if she couldn't hold his gaze, "I have been wanting to talk to you."

Luke shook his head sadly, "I can't imagine what we would have to say to each other now."

"Luke...you know that I am a very shy girl," Hannah said in a shaky voice, "And I have let my fear get the better of me far too many times. I almost let it destroy what we had together. But Luke...I can't let that happen."

David's eyes got large as he realized that Luke must be the ex-beau that Hannah had told him about.

"I love you, Luke," Hannah announced resolutely, "I love you and I still want to be your wife...if you can ever find it in your heart to have me."

David watched Luke and held his breath, hoping that he would agree.

Stepping forward, Luke reached out and took Hannah in his arms, "I love you too, Hannah!" He exclaimed as he cupped her face in his hands, "I have always loved you and I always will." Turning to look at Lovina, he quickly tried to explain, "Lovina, I hope that you understand..."

Lovina smiled broadly as she wrapped her arms around David's waist, "It is fine, Luke. I think that things are exactly the way that they are supposed to be!"

Epilogue

Standing together at the kitchen sink, Lovina and David watched as a group of children played outside in their front yard.

"Look at those crazy things," Lovina muttered as she noticed her daughter trying to climb a tree.

"Just like us when we were little," David announced.

Lovina looked up at him and smirked, "*Jah* – and I think our little girl might have a crush on the neighbor boy, as well."

David and Lovina had now been married for ten years and had three children of their own. It had been a double wedding shared with Hannah and Luke, who decided to move to Kentucky so that Luke would continue to enjoy a steady stream of work.

David and Lovina had built their house behind his parents' place and, to their surprise, Hannah and Luke had bought a piece of farm land right across the creek.

Their children played together and it wouldn't be any surprise if someday those same children would grow up to marry one another.

David smiled broadly and gathered his wife up in his arms.

"I'm glad I went to Indiana that summer," he announced as he reached out to push a strand of her brown hair back from her face, "Because that summer showed me how much I need you in my life."

Bending over, he gave her a gentle kiss.

Life truly was as David and Lovina had always imagined it – and they were happier than they ever could have guessed possible.

THE END